Tentacles Numbing

A Novel

Shome Dasgupta

for

deep

Tentacles Numbing

1

Ravi was haunted by the daydreams of his own hanging. It was in the evening, in a ghost town setting during the time of cowboys and saloons, and there was no one else around, but he could hear a crowd's murmur. It was the murmur he heard when he would fall asleep as a young child in the middle of one of his parents' social gatherings. He hung there, wearing a T-shirt, socks, and jeans, and he slightly swayed back and forth in the still air. A cowboy hat lay on the wooden boards below him. These were his daydreams. There was no beginning, and there was no end—just the dead middle.

At night, Ravi thought about sleeping—a pure sleep where he was lost as soon as he closed his eyes, and when he woke up, he did so without a yawn. He wished to open his eyes, relaxed, and gathered like a Zen Master, ready to start the day. These were just dreams, though. He was fulfilling his reveries—he just hung.

Earlier in Ravi's young life, when he couldn't sleep, he would exercise to tire himself, or he would read a book with the Weather Channel on. Now, when he did sit-ups and jumping jacks, he coughed a smoker's cough, and if he tried to read a book with the Weather Channel on, he would finish the book or could state the weather and temperature for almost every state in America for the next day, perhaps even the next week.

Last night, Ravi switched from watching the Weather Channel to viewing various late-night infomercials. He was fascinated with these industrial-strength vacuum cleaners, blenders, and knives. He was even more interested in the hosts or inventors of these instruments. They seemed driven, and confident, and they all had glimmers in their pupils. Years had passed since the last time he had such a gleam in his own eyes. He didn't have any spark to do anything anymore, except simply make it through the day.

Ravi didn't do much. He kept to himself, avoided most conversations, and thought a lot about the past. This kept him from moving forward. He knew this, and yet he still chose not to look ahead or try to find that sense of joy that most people search for as they grow up. Love? Nothing. He would have to look it up in the dictionary just to get a general idea of the concept. Laughter? Nothing. If he laughed now, his body would start to tremor in shock. Stimulation? Nothing. He was stagnant like a rusted fire hydrant. Feelings? Nothing. Numb.

He'd been kicked in the face several times. This happened to him once during P.E. class while playing basketball. He had lost all sensation in his nose and mouth, and he didn't regain any feeling until five minutes later. It was the same thing as going to the dentist to get a cavity filled—how the dentist would stick a needle in his gums so he didn't feel the drilling, and after drooling water or milk or a bowl of cereal for ten minutes, he would get his mouth back. He was kicked in the face when his parents were killed. Again when his brother left him. It happened one more time when he realized that his brother was a drunk. He'd been hit so hard in the face so many times, that he just couldn't get any sensation back. He was living his life at the dentist's office. It was all gone. And this feeling or lack of feeling had crept from his mouth to his brain, and down into his feet. He was just a void.

2

"Twyaneraurus wex. Look."
"Indeed."
"It can be as long as a school bus."
"Really?"
"Yeah. And they can have feathers."
"Feathers? No."
"Do you know what they're related to?"
"Who?"
"Guess, Vavi."
"Let's see. Maybe an alligator or a crocodile?"
"Chicken."
"Chickens!"
"And ostriches!"
"Ostriches!"
"I love dinosaurs."
"I know you do, Ravi."
"I love you, Vavi."
"I love you, Ravi."
"You want to play some soccer with me?"
"Let's do it. I'll meet you in the backyard in about five minutes. Dress warm."
"Got it."
"And Ravi?"
"Yeah."
"I love you."
"Dinosaurs."

3

Ravi was starting his shift at the grocery store—from 10 pm to 8 am. Annie had just closed the flower department, and she was on her way out. The only drawback of working the night shift was that he wasn't able to work with Annie, because the flower department was only open until ten at night.

Annie. She and Ravi were kind of the same. They liked their space, their privacy. She was his age—twenty-four—and she had lived in Seattle her whole life and had graduated from North Seattle Community College. Annie had been working at the store for two years. Her mother was around, but her father had left them for another woman when Annie was thirteen. Ravi once asked her about it.

"I'm glad he left. He wasn't any good anyway."

"Do you miss him at all?"

"Only for my mom's sake, I guess. Other than that, he's nothing to me."

Like Ravi, she didn't have any friends except for whatever relationships formed at the grocery store. Her brown hair was tangled, and she didn't wear any cosmetics, which revealed the dark shadows beneath her brown eyes. She smiled now and then, but her mind seemed to be preoccupied with something else. She usually wore long-sleeve shirts with scuffed-up green tennis shoes and a slew of bracelets around each arm.

Ravi believed that she wanted to change her life. He thought that she was struggling to be happy, and when he did get a glimpse of her cheerful side, it was like watching a hundred hot air balloons, as colorful as the bracelets around her wrists, soaring through the sky. It was a sight to see. She was not the "life sucks, I always want to be depressed and dark" kind of person. She just hadn't found her way yet. Ravi and Annie went through the same motions every day, despised it, yet did nothing about it.

It was a Sunday night, which meant that business was going to be slow, and a lot of stocking up would have to be done for the upcoming week. After two hours of placing canned juices, jelly jars, and cereal boxes on the shelves, Ravi took a fifteen-minute break and went outside for a smoke. Annie was sitting on the bench outside the grocery store.

"You on your fifteen?" she asked.

"Yeah. But what are you doing?"

"Bored," she said. "Thought you would be taking a break soon. I just got here."

Ravi took off his apron so that the customers wouldn't see him smoking and representing LVS Grocers at the same time, then sat down next to her. It was the first time Ravi had seen her outside of work, even though they were just sitting directly in front of the store. The parking lot light gave her a magical princess look: pale skin, brown eyes, and a rounded nose—a nose he wanted to kiss every time he saw it. The night covered one side of her face, but the other half shone. He looked up for a second and noticed the half-moon. She wore a maroon skirt, a black spaghetti-strapped shirt, and sandals. Her fingernails were painted dark blue. Her brown hair was tied in a bun, and the rainbow-colored assortment of bracelets decorated her wrists.

"Going out or something?" Ravi asked.

"No," Annie said. "Why? Do I look too dressed up or something?"

"No, no. Not at all. You look nice."

"Thanks," she said.

They both took a couple of drags before she spoke again.

"How's the shift?"

"Slow."

"Are you still having those fucked up dreams?" she asked.

Annie was the only person who knew about his constant daydreams. He had told her about it because he thought it would help her out—that it would let her know that she was not the only one who lived in a numb, surreal, zombie-like world. She also knew about the death of his parents, and about his brother.

"Still dreaming about it," Ravi said. "I'm getting tired of it—no matter how hard I try not to. It becomes clearer and clearer each time."

She nodded her head and looked out into the parking lot, revealing a series of small hoop earrings going from the top of her ear to the lobe.

"You'll be okay," she said.

"Yeah. And you?"

"What about me?"

"How are you doing?" Ravi asked. "I haven't seen you in a few days. How are things?"

"The same. You know. Everything is just nothing."

"What's going on tonight?" he asked. "You doing anything?"

"Laundry. I must be here early tomorrow because the truck is coming."

They flicked their cigarettes onto the sidewalk and stood up.

"Catch you later," he said.

"Yeah," Annie replied. "Don't have too much fun at work."

"You know me."

He wanted to ask her out—for dinner, or maybe a movie—but he wasn't sure if it would work. He'd never really asked anyone out before. It was hard to get any kind of vibe from her, but then again, she'd never waited outside the store for him before.

"Annie."

She was in the middle of the parking lot as he stood in the middle of the sliding doors. She turned around.

"Nothing."

She smiled. He could see it with the help of the parking lot light. She continued to walk, and Ravi went back to work.

Randy was stocking apples when Ravi asked him if the chocolate-covered pretzels went in the candy or chips section. He threw his apples to the ground, grabbed Ravi by the neck, and pushed him against a shelf full of water bottles. He tried to strangle Ravi. He shouted and screamed, but not directly at Ravi.

"What is it about my life?" Randy asked. "What is it about my life? What?"

It was more of a release of pent-up energy, and Ravi just happened to be around him when it happened. Ravi saw a rope. He saw the wooden boards below. He could feel the rope tighten around his neck, and the sun, in its descent, gave him sympathy. He wanted to tell it thanks, but he just hung out instead. Ravi didn't react. He didn't push Randy away—he was too busy dreaming about the ghost town. He was too numb.

After about a minute, Randy finished his fit and looked around. No customers or employees were around. Randy was a portly man with balding hair. He didn't wear glasses but squinted whenever he talked to someone or read something. Overall, he was a nice guy.

Ravi rubbed his fingers around his neck to soothe the

burning. Randy rubbed his eyes with one hand while scratching his head with the other.

"Sorry Ravi," he said. "Having a bad day. I understand if you tell Mr. Riley about this. I deserve it."

"Not at all. I understand."

"They go in the candy section," he said. "I'll be in the back if you need anything else."

Randy walked away, and Ravi took the box of pretzels to the candy section. The bottles of water were left rolling on the ground. It was not the first time Randy had had a fit, but it was the first time he'd physically handled anyone. He worked sixty hours a week on average. Ravi thought he would go crazy, too, if he worked those kinds of days.

A few hours later, a homeless woman walked into the store. Ravi tried not to make eye contact with her, but that didn't make him invisible. His shift was about to end, and he was just finishing placing paper towels in Aisle G.

Why are the dogs dying?" she asked.

She had red eyes and wore a long black coat, a pair of bright-red sweatpants, a black T-shirt, and a black ski cap. From underneath the hat, long scraggly gray hair stuck out, clumped together.

"I'm not sure," Ravi replied.

"Don't you care?" she asked.

"I care, but what can I do?"

"You can leave. Leave this earth and save the dogs. They cry for you."

"I can't," I said. "My brother."

"Find him," she replied. "And the dogs are dying."

She walked away. Ravi kept his distance, and then followed her for a few seconds until she walked outside.

"Twinkle, Twinkle" kept playing in his head, but not with the correct words: "Twinkle, twinkle, little star, don't you know my head is at war? Down below the sky, I hang.

Won't you twinkle and listen to me sing? Twinkle, twinkle, little star, I don't wonder who you are. Stop your shining from afar, and let me hang from this bar." *What a lullaby*, he thought.

After he finished his shift at the grocery store, Ravi went to the hardware store and bought some rope. He had been thinking about doing this throughout the night, and he couldn't help himself. He stood there in the middle of Aisle P-3, sampling the several types of ropes. He looked to the ceiling and saw the large pipe supporting the light fixture, running from one end of the store to the other, and he pictured hanging himself from it.

Back at the apartment, Ravi tied the rope in a noose, and he kept it at the foot of his bed. He was trying to attack his reverie instead of hiding from it. The rope was some sort of pillow. It gave reality to the daydream. It made something concrete out of what was intangible.

4

Ravi and his older brother Vavi used to play marbles when they were much younger. Ravi was seven when they started playing, and Vavi was fifteen. This was ten years before he started dreaming of hanging himself.

They weren't really the competitive type, the two of them, so Vavi would let him win most of the games, but sometimes the older brother would win just to make it look like he was really trying the whole time. Ravi didn't care about winning or losing—he just liked being around his brother, and he liked looking at the different sizes and colors of the marbles. Hearing the quiet click noise when one ball hit another was like falling asleep to a lullaby—it caressed the ears, softened the eyes, and rubbed the back. Vavi had a dark black marble. It wasn't transparent, except for certain parts where there was white and gray cloud-like material floating around. It looked like one of those photographs found in a science textbook, in the astronomy section, where the chapter would be talking about the mysteries of the universe. Vavi ended up giving Ravi the marble as a birthday gift because he saw his younger brother's eyes filled with wonder every time he took it out of the box. Ravi kept it wrapped in a soft cloth, resting in the same shoebox they had used when they were younger.

Vavi lived in downtown Seattle, which was about a fifteen-minute walk from where Ravi stayed. He lived on the streets—he was a semi-drunkard homeless man, and yet, Ravi still looked up to him. He tried to get Vavi to move in with him. He tried to tell his brother to get a job at the grocery store, and he tried telling him that sleeping on the streets was no way to live, but Vavi didn't listen.

"This is my home."

"How?"

"This is my home."

Ravi wondered if it was a pride thing. *Vavi needs my help*, Ravi thought, but Vavi didn't want to show his younger brother that he was struggling. He wanted to be the older brother, and perhaps he believed that this meant that he should be helping Ravi out and not the other way around.

He became homeless while Ravi started dreaming of wrapping a noose around his neck. This was shortly after their parents were killed. They were living with their mother's sister then, and not too long after they'd moved in with her, Vavi unexpectedly took off. He didn't tell his aunt or his brother where he was going, but he left a note on the microwave which read, "I'll be okay."

None of them took the tragedy of their parents' deaths too well, and none of them had fully recovered from it still. Ravi didn't need a psychologist to tell him this. He barely made it through his last year of high school, let alone life. For college, it took him five years to graduate with a 2.0 GPA, attached to several school probations. He ended up with a degree in History and contemplated suicide regularly. He assumed the thought entered his brother's mind, as well. They'd had a close relationship with their parents. They all went through intense arguments and tantrums, but in the end, things were always going to be okay.

One month before their parents were killed, Vavi had just graduated from the University of Washington at Seattle with an undergraduate degree in Psychology. He had nothing to hold him back, so he left. Ravi didn't blame Vavi for leaving, but he wished his brother would have stayed home for a bit longer. He loved his aunt, but his older brother was the one he looked to for guidance. Though he was eight years older than Ravi, he was his best friend. Vavi looked after him just as Mother and Father would. The tragedy greatly shifted things—Vavi barely spoke anymore, nor did Ravi remember seeing him laugh or smile. He kept to himself in the attic of their aunt's home, reading by candlelight.

"What are you doing up here?"

"Just reading."

"Do you want to play Uno?"

"Maybe next time."

Ravi felt helpless. When Vavi needed someone, they were dead, and he was just a clueless freshman in high school. Vavi needed to take care of himself, and for him to do this, he moved away and sought out the streets as his new home.

Ravi's ghost town daydreams and sleepless nights hadn't ceased since his parents' deaths. He'd been working at the grocery store off Harvard Avenue, which was across the street from where he had lived for almost six years. It wasn't too fun of a job, but he liked the smell of lettuce, tomatoes, cauliflower, and celery all meshed into one. He usually had the day schedule, but on those fortunate days when the manager assigned some graveyard shifts for him, he didn't have to worry about not being able to sleep.

He spent much of his time in parks, and he frequently visited Bruce Lee's grave, though he had never seen any of his movies. Lakeview Cemetery had become some sort of a comforting chasm for Ravi. It was his hiding spot. It was his silent movie. When the wind blew and the leaves rustled, this gentle tugging and releasing—the gravestones, trees, flowers, crickets, and weather—they all came into homeostasis. When the sun entered this silent garden, slowly and cozily, he could easily doze on one of the benches and let the dead lull him to sleep. Ravi had yet to visit his parents' marble homes since the morning of the funeral, but he felt more comfortable sitting in front of Bruce Lee. Next to his grave was a small, dirty one, half-hidden underneath a dying bush. He pushed aside some of the twigs and brushed the dirt off the grave so people could see his name—Matthew Nessle. Apart from the occasional ant, Ravi assumed that no one visited Bruce Lee's neighbor, so he bought some sunflowers from the grocery store and placed them next to this person's grave.

Ravi would get the sunflowers from Annie. She was the only one Ravi really talked to at the grocery store. They smoked together on their breaks, and when they did talk, they talked about trivial things, like crazy customers, aisle spills, and the front covers of the tabloids.

Once, on a slow day, they started throwing tomatoes at each other. This could have easily gotten them fired, but Randy was having such a difficult day that he decided to get in on the action to let out some aggression himself, but he used lettuce instead. It was just the three of them working that night. Soon after, the district manager, Mr. Riley, had them install video cameras within the store, so that one night marked the first and last vegetable fight. Mr. Riley was an obese man who wasn't that nice. His personality was accented by this stinging smell of vinegar that seemed to come from his neck—a combination of his sweat and cologne mixed. When Mr. Riley asked Randy about the tomatoes and lettuce, after the inventory looked a bit thin, Randy just shrugged his shoulders.

"Must have been some troublemaker making some trouble."

Mr. Riley called Annie and Ravi into the office, as well, and they both stared at the floor while he pinned them with questions. They both quietly lied to him.

"Maybe ghosts," Annie said.

"I didn't see anything," Ravi said. "I didn't feel anything, but maybe there was an earthquake."

"Maybe an earthquake of ghosts," Annie said.

Mr. Riley knew they were all lying, and despite his acerbic personality, he let them all slide for some reason—Mr. Riley didn't have any proof, nor would anyone else have wanted to manage the store at the time.

5

Auntie tried her best to keep the brothers happy. They knew that she herself was struggling, but she never openly showed it to them. When they were around her, she was smiling and well dressed, either in a neatly folded sari or a long dress. Her hair was tied tightly in a bun, and the only cosmetics she used were red lipstick and black eyeliner. She smelled of India—incense, and curry because those two things were constantly being used or cooked in her house. The brothers had to sneak around to find her in the bedroom, sitting on the bed, crying silently while she held a framed photograph of herself and her sister.

"I miss you, Didi."

They saw Auntie do this on a regular basis—weekly, every Sunday, like she was going to church. Despite seeing this, neither Vavi nor Ravi made any effort to help her out, to show her some sympathy, to let her know that they were grateful for all that she had done. After Vavi left, Ravi rarely talked to her, mainly keeping to his bed, listening to music, or reading while thinking about the past.

One Sunday morning, on a bright day in March, Auntie asked Ravi to go to the park with her for a walk. She had asked him several times before, and all those times he had told her no, though it killed Ravi to say so, and he was sure it saddened her, as well. But this time Ravi said yes.

"Really?"

"Sure. Let's go."

"Really?"

"It'll be nice, Auntie."

He was just about to graduate high school, and it was his way of saying thanks for everything—a walk at the park for taking care of him, loving him, and supporting him since the death of Mother and Father.

She held his hand as they walked—as runners ran by, as dogs sniffed to mark their territory, as children played Frisbee or baseball—and they had a good talk, covering his high school career, his future with college, and girls. It was the talk they should have had every day, and Ravi felt bad for summarizing it all up on one Sunday morning.

"I just wanted to let you know," Auntie said, "that your parents loved you and Vavi so much, no matter how strict they were. They constantly talked about you both when they were visiting, laughing and smiling."

"I know," he said.

That was all that Ravi could say to that.

"Do you think you'll find your brother?" she asked.

Neither Auntie nor Ravi had seen Vavi since he had left. He never kept in touch, but Auntie didn't really seem to worry, either. She somehow knew that he was still alive. Sometimes Ravi wondered whether she really knew where Vavi was staying, but she never revealed anything. It was like she knew that, one day, he would be back.

"I'm not sure," he said. "Maybe he'll find me."

Two weeks after their walk, Ravi left her home and moved into his own apartment across from the grocery store. And Vavi found Ravi while the younger brother was looking for him. Ravi was walking around downtown when he heard Vavi call his name. Who knew how many times Ravi had walked past him, not seeing or recognizing him?

"It's about time," Vavi said.

He had a beer bottle in one hand and a pack of smokes in the other. He didn't get up to hug Ravi, though it had been so long since they had seen each other. It hurt inside when Ravi saw him on the sidewalk, wearing torn clothes and smelling of urine. He could feel his chest sink in and the emptiness in his stomach magnify. Ravi tried hard not to show any sorrow and acted as happily as possible. He sat down next to Vavi and patted him on the shoulder, and Vavi did the same to him. That was the best they could do at that moment. They didn't talk much—a little bit about Auntie and what Ravi had been doing, and that was about it. He barely looked at Ravi, and he always had a grin on his face like he knew some secret about the world. Vavi told Ravi that he would be working on a screenplay soon and that Ravi should visit him more often.

"I'm always here," Vavi said.

6

Ravi had just finished visiting Bruce Lee's grave and went to a café to sit and read for a bit. Bill needed a shift to make rent, so Ravi gave it to him, and he didn't mind having an unexpected day off from the aisles.

When he reached the coffee shop, he saw Annie sitting at an outside table, sipping an iced tea and reading a magazine.

"Annie."

She looked up but didn't give any kind of expression.

"Annie."

She looked up again and acted like she didn't recognize him.

"Hey, it's me. Ravi."

The blank expression on her face changed back to her normal look.

"You okay?" he asked.

She nodded her head and continued to read her magazine. He sat down next to her and put his hand on her shoulder.

"What's wrong?"

"I'm lost," she said. "I don't know what to do anymore. I'm tired of my life."

"I understand."

"It's like I feel like there is no purpose to my life. Like I don't belong in this world."

"I know how you feel," he said.

"Do you?" she asked.

"The only reason I get up is so I can get my brother to stop being homeless. Otherwise, I don't think I could still go on either."

Annie stopped sniffling and gazed into her iced tea.

"Maybe we don't belong here," Ravi said, "but since we are here, let's try to have some fun."

He was being a hypocrite. He didn't know how to have fun anymore—it had been too long.

"It's like I'm always in a daze," Annie said. "And each day, I become increasingly dazed. I feel like one day, you will be able to pinch me, and I wouldn't feel a thing."

She started to cry, and she tried to speak at the same time, but Ravi couldn't make any sense of it. He handed her a napkin and waited for her to calm down. The people sitting at the table next to them looked at her. He looked back at them, and they quickly looked away when they saw Ravi. He had never seen Annie vulnerable like this.

"Yesterday," he said, "when I woke up to get ready for work, I walked into a corner table. I didn't realize that I was bleeding until a customer said something. The blood had trickled down, covering most of my left leg. I felt the pain and all, but the thing is, I didn't even bother to check my knee."

"So, what do we do?" she asked. "I mean, look at me being selfish and crying and asking for attention when you've had to deal with the death of your parents, and your brother and all."

"You become used to it," he replied. "There's nothing else I do, but just become accustomed to it. Routine after routine. You feel kind of nothing after a while, you know, like Novocain."

Annie looked at Ravi.

"I'm sorry for all of this," she said.

"Not at all."

"Do you think Scarlett Johansson is hot?" Annie asked.

"Sure," Ravi said. "I think she's really pretty."

"You know some people have told me that I look like

her. And not just guys, but girls, too."

"Well," he said, "you're pretty, too."

Ravi thought she needed to hear that. Sometimes he wished someone would tell him that he was pretty, too.

They sat and talked at the café. The weather changed from sunny to cloudy, and a loud thunderstorm came. They didn't move inside, though. The breeze was nice in the summertime, and the lightning was fascinating to see. As the thunderstorm settled, they both became silent and watched and listened to the weather. They smoked cigarette after cigarette and let the winds carry their smoke down the sidewalk.

Once the rain had subsided, Ravi walked to downtown Seattle and found Vavi. He was at his usual spot—just outside his favorite coffee shop, Beans. He was wearing his favorite gray shirt, with the word "Om" written several times on it in dark black Sanskrit. It was in a concentric pattern until it got to the center, where there was just one "Om."

The employees at Beans didn't give him any trouble about loitering. They all liked him, and Ravi guessed he couldn't really see why they would not like him. Vavi kept to himself, and he didn't disturb the pedestrians too much, but by the end of the day, his smile and his ability to have intelligent conversations afforded him enough money for a cup of coffee and a bagel or two for dinner. Every now and then, the baristas would give him a free cup and some pastries that would have been thrown away if Vavi didn't take them.

"Just in time for dinner, Ravi. Would you like some of my bagel?"

"How are you?"

"It's blueberry."

He smiled—a smile composed of the remnants of

happiness. Glassy eyes and a wavering head revealed to Ravi that he was drunk. The smell of beer emanating from him made Ravi breathe through his mouth. Homelessness had finally taken its toll on Vavi's appearance. Tangled lumps of hair poked out from under his ski cap. It used to be brown, but it was all cobwebs now. His beard was thick, unkempt, and a haven for crumbs. Dark, large bags underneath his eyes led to wrinkles. Ravi used to marvel at his brother's physique whenever they went swimming or when he was working in the yard—he just couldn't get over the idea of Vavi's physical appearance back then. His calves used to be well-defined and neatly packed against his bones. His thighs, large and oblong, used to bulge without effort. The muscles on the back of his neck leading down to his shoulders had accented his broad back. What once was a sturdy and stocky build, built for football and track, had diminished into a concave stomach and a bent body.

"You need anything?" Ravi asked.

He shook his head and took a bite of his bagel: "Of course not. I'm fine. How are things going?"

Ravi wanted to tell him about his dreams, but he didn't want to bother him with his own problems while Vavi was living on the streets. Ravi just wished his brother would move in with him.

"Yeah," Ravi said, "why don't you move in with me?"

Vavi swallowed and sipped his coffee.

"You know what I'm going to ans—"

"Yeah, I know. I just had to ask."

Ravi looked at the sky and thought about how he could change the subject. He saw a cloud in the shape of a cat—it had pointy ears and a long tail that eventually thinned out into the air.

"Oh. Do you know anything about dying dogs? Some lady came in the other day asking me about dying dogs."

"Nope. Haven't heard of that one yet, but I'll let you know if I find out."

Ravi sat down next to his brother and leaned back against the bricks of the building.

"You don't get lonely out here?" he asked.

"How can I get lonely when I'm constantly surrounded by these beautiful people?"

He was lonely. Ravi was lonely. They were both lonely without each other, without their parents, without their minds. But Ravi left it at that. He looked at Vavi's bag—it was the only thing Vavi kept care of, even more than himself. In it were a couple of imperishable items, mainly soup, which he kept for those days when he might not find much to eat. There was also a stack of paper, meticulously kept together by a large clip.

"How's the script coming?" Ravi asked.

"Working on it. Working on it."

That was all he would say to Ravi about the screenplay. He didn't want to let Ravi know what it was really about, but Vavi did tell him that it centered on a monstrous jellyfish.

"You're drunk," Ravi said.

"That may be, but I'm still living, right?"

Ravi couldn't remember the last time he had seen his brother sober.

Vavi started talking about movies. Every now and then, he managed to sneak in and watch a movie at the theater. Sometimes the employees helped him. Other times he snuck in while others walked out during the end credits and found a hiding spot until the next show began. He was talking about a movie he saw that starred Matt Damon, and Ravi was trying hard to listen to him, but he faded away and saw himself hanging again. It was quiet. The sun was still there, and the wooden boards smelled of fresh varnish. No one else was there. Just Ravi, rocking in the air a bit, with his eyes closed and his hands by his side. The cowboy hat, this time, was on the other side of him.

7

He was back at the apartment. He should be tired. He should be exhausted. He was both, yet he didn't sleep. Ravi stared at the rope that was wrapped around the neck of the lamp in his bedroom. His room was bare. He had nothing in it but a bed, a bedside table with a lamp that hadn't been turned on in months, and a television. He kept his place dimly lit—the lights in the living room and the kitchen were off, but he always kept the bathroom light on. It was the brightest light in the apartment, and it was a reliable source for lighting the whole place just the way he liked it. It made him feel like he was in a hotel or at a hospital.

He thought about the time his parents took him to the park to feed the ducks. Vavi was at a friend's house, so he didn't go, but he had already gone several times before— that was Ravi's first time there. A loaf of bread was under his father's arm, and he held an umbrella with the same hand just in case it rained. He wore a khaki raincoat and one of those hats that golfers wore a long time ago. He always wore slacks. Mother wore a blue dress with white dots, and it came down just above her mid-calves. Both his parents were slim. Mother had long black silky Indian hair, and she held herself humbly, with grace. She would smile when she scolded Vavi or Ravi. She didn't work after she gave birth to Vavi, but before that, she was an assistant at the public library. After her death, her library was all boxed up at her sister's place. Ravi told himself that once he lived in a big enough place, he would have bookshelves to fully display her collection. Father was a CPA for a private firm and made around $300,000 a year which allowed them to live quite comfortably. He was just as nice as Mother, though he didn't smile at the boys when they were being scolded. But soon after each scolding or argument, he would give them a hug and a kiss on the forehead, and then he would ask them to help him with something, like changing light bulbs, even though they didn't need changing, or cleaning the kitchen, even though the kitchen had just been cleaned.

That day at the park was a normal spring day—sunny, with a slight chill. The grass was long, dark green, and sprayed with bits and pieces of sunlight. Mother made sure to keep Ravi out from under the tree shades so he wouldn't catch a cold. The ducks, looking like the ones found in Mother Goose stories—bright white with polished yellow beaks and soft black eyes—were not nice that day. They weren't too cooperative. The family each took a slice of bread and crushed it using their hands to make crumbs. Ravi sprinkled the breadcrumbs onto the grass, and the ducks quacked and waddled to the feast. They pecked and pecked and looked at each other in astonishment. Mother fed them next, and they did the same, but when Father dropped some pieces of bread, the ducks decided to peck not at the food, but at Father's leg. They surrounded him, quacking—their voices sounded like they were full of scorn. At first, Father laughed and kept throwing more breadcrumbs, but once the pecking and quacking increased, he started to run. The ducks followed. He opened his umbrella to shield himself from the beaks, but they pierced through. Father started to run at a faster speed until the ducks couldn't keep up with him. But they continued to stay in a huddle and stare at him, and with their quacks, they seemed to be telling him not to come back. Mother was laughing so much that tears were forming, and she said her stomach was starting to hurt. Ravi had tears, as well, but he was crying, worried that Father was going to get eaten by the birds. Father ended up throwing the umbrella away, and he gave the remaining slices of bread to Mother. She happily fed the ducks, while Ravi looked at Father who raised his pant legs to see his shins covered in small dots of red. Some dripped, and some were just signs of bruising. Despite this incident, they did go back to the park, and Vavi went with them, as well. And the ducks were nice from then on, but just in case, Father wore Vavi's soccer shin guards underneath his slacks.

Ravi didn't cry as he thought about those times at the park. He grabbed the lamp and switched it on and off, on and off, and caressed the rope wrapped around its neck, feeling its strands at certain spots where one cord was bound with another. It was a thick rope, tough and rugged, made of polyester, making it unable to stretch. It cost only fifteen dollars to fulfill his dreams. He leaned on the window sill and watched the world twirl before him.

8

When he felt lonely, Ravi's senses heightened. It was like he was blind and his hearing abilities had become much more acute, or he was deaf and his eyes had become sharper. He was sitting in the Coffee Hut, sipping a mocha, and without looking, he sensed that the couple at the table next to him was in the middle of an argument as they muttered to each other. With just a glance, he saw the guy sit back in his seat with his arms folded while the lady sat with her legs crossed away from him. Her face sagged—her eyebrows, her eyes, her lips, and her cheeks. The guy rolled his eyes and sighed and mumbled under his breath, "Well, if you wouldn't keep such tight control over me, maybe I wouldn't come home so late." His shoelaces were untied, and her shoes looked like they were too small for her as the tops of her feet were red and scrunched up.

At the table on the other side of them sat a family—a mother, a father, and a young boy. The boy held a Spiderman toy in his hand, and he made these whooshing noises as he guided it through the air, spitting and shouting the superhero's name. The parents were holding each other's hands, and their bodies were tilted toward each other as they whispered about tonight when they would be alone in their bedroom.

A teenage girl sat at the other end of the café. She was talking on her cell phone with one hand tapping the tabletop, and her legs were constantly shifting about. She scowled as she turned her head to the floor and screamed at her father for not letting her go to a party this weekend. There was a coffee stain on the wall right behind her.

Ravi noticed all this while looking out the window.

As the boy continued to play with his Spiderman toy, Ravi thought about when he and Vavi were younger, playing at a friend's house. His name was Vikram, and his family was a part of the Indian community which was how the families had met. Vikram was three years older than Ravi—he wore a gold chain around his neck, magnifying the dark color of his skin. His parents were doctors—the father a surgeon, and the mother a pediatrician. They lived in a castle-like house on top of a hill. Ravi used to imagine a moat surrounding the house, with a dragon flying above it. It was a gray brick house, two stories, and he had been in at least six rooms of the castle.

Vikram was protective of his toys. He kept them all organized in red baskets in his bedroom. Each container was appointed for action heroes, cars and trucks, Legos, or video games. He didn't let Ravi touch his toys, but Vavi was allowed to play with them, even though he was more into reading books by that time. Ravi sat on the carpet as he watched Vavi and Vikram play. Vavi pretended to be having fun, just enough to appease Vikram.

One day, while the parents were having lunch together at the castle, Vikram, Vavi, and Ravi went to the backyard to jump on the trampoline. As Ravi was trying to get onto the trampoline, Vikram pushed him off, causing him to fall onto the grass, on his back. He was a bit winded, but his head hurt the most when it hit the ground.

"You can't jump," Vikram said. "You're too young. Come on, Vavi. You and I can jump."

Vavi got onto the trampoline and nudged Vikram just enough to make him jump off the trampoline and onto the grass. Vavi hopped off, as well. As Ravi stood up, he saw Vavi's eyes were narrow. His brow drooped, and he was grinding his teeth. He pointed his finger at Vikram.

"Don't you ever push my brother. Ever," Vavi said.

"You're a spoiled brat. You need to learn how to be nice to people, otherwise, you'll get yourself in a lot of trouble. Quit being so mean."

Vikram didn't look at Vavi. He just stared at the ground, rubbing the back of his head with his hand. He didn't look at the brothers as he got back onto the trampoline and started to jump and do flips. Vavi put his hand on the back of Ravi's neck and guided him inside. They went into the living room and watched *The Simpsons,* and Vikram came inside and asked if both would like to jump on the trampoline. Vavi smiled and said yes, and they all went back outside. Vikram helped Ravi onto the trampoline. It was the first time Ravi could remember Vavi sticking up for him. He knew Vavi loved him, and that his older brother always played with him and kept him company, but when Vavi pushed Vikram off the trampoline and told him to be nice, Ravi had never felt such a strong love before.

Later on, that night, when they were back at their own house, Ravi couldn't sleep. He went to Vavi's room, where Vavi was in bed, reading.

"Thanks for earlier today," Ravi said.

"You're too nice of a guy," Vavi said. "And don't ever change. Never. But being so kind allows you to get hurt more because people will take advantage of you. Push you aside. I'm not always going to be there for you, so you need to learn how to stick up for yourself. Now go to sleep."

They didn't see Vikram for another month until their parents had a get-together for the Indian community. The other parents found babysitters for their kids or their children were old enough to look after themselves, so Vikram was the only child who Vavi and Ravi had to keep company. Ravi let him play with his toys without any hesitation, and Vikram was content with playing with his spaceships for most of the night. He told Ravi thanks.

Vikram told him that he could come over to his house any time to play with his toys, and he patted Ravi on the back.

Nearing the end of the night, they all decided to play football in the backyard, which made both Ravi and Vikram tire quickly, but the party was not anywhere near finishing. Vikram went to Ravi's room and fell asleep on the carpet. The brothers went to the living room, where Vavi talked with the adults. Ravi was amazed at how his brother held himself—shaking people's hands, nodding his head, and talking like a grown-up. Ravi would go around, as well, and shake their hands, trying to be like his brother.

Ravi remembered when he sat on the sofa, his head leaning against his father's shoulder, his eyes slowly closing. He tried hard to keep them open, to stay up with the adults and Vavi, but he drifted away to the humming of his parents' social gathering. When his eyes finally opened, Vavi was carrying him to his bedroom so he could sleep properly in his bed. Vavi rubbed his head and whispered to him, "I'll see you in the morning."

Vavi was a secretive character—he was always thinking and rarely talking. He didn't have any posters, and he didn't watch television much—only to keep Ravi company more than for his own entertainment. He didn't invite school friends over to the house, and he rarely went over to his friends' houses. Ravi knew his brother's interest was in books because he kept them displayed on his bookshelf. He knew that Vavi liked the music of Nirvana, Pearl Jam, Pink Floyd, Radiohead, and Bob Dylan, and their father had introduced him to the music of Ravi Shankar, Rabindranath Tagore, and Shakti. His room was always clean: the bedsheets were neatly tucked, the clothes were all folded neatly in the dresser, and he kept everything organized on his desk—the stapler on the top right corner, the notebooks perfectly centered, and on the left side, he left space for textbooks and reading books. He didn't like Ravi handling his books, because he was obsessed with not having any creases on the spines. This didn't matter to Ravi, because he was too young to understand what he was reading, but if he ever wanted to look at the picture on the cover or thumb through the pages to learn the more complicated words, Vavi always held the book for him.

One night, when Ravi couldn't sleep, he walked to Vavi's room to see if he was still awake. He was in bed, reading a book, and next to him, underneath the covers, was a slight bulge.

"Why are you still up?" Vavi asked.

"Too much Coke."

"Well, come sit."

Ravi sat at the foot of his bed. Vavi's eyes were red and glassy. His head looked like it was barely connected to his shoulders, as it rocked and swayed. He closed his book and placed it on the bedside table.

"What are you reading?" Ravi asked.

"Just started *Siddhartha*. Shouldn't take too long to finish. You should read it when I'm done."

Vavi rubbed his forehead and then his face.

"You don't look so well," Ravi said.

"I'm okay."

From underneath the covers, he pulled out a bottle of vodka and took a sip.

"Don't tell Mother and Father, alright?" he said.

"I won't."

"And don't let me ever catch you doing this," Vavi said.

"You won't."

He took another sip and hid the bottle underneath the covers again.

"How come you're drinking?"

"I don't really know."

"Are you drunk?"

"I don't really know."

"Do you do this a lot?" Ravi asked.

"Not really. But I've been doing it a lot lately. I enjoy it while I read at night, and it helps me go to sleep, too."

"What's wrong?"

Ravi felt like Vavi's bedroom was tucked away from the rest of the world. They were in a vacuum of some sort, where nothing else existed like they were exiled from all society.

"Nothing," Vavi said. "I just felt like I needed a drink. That's all."

9

A week had passed since Ravi talked to Annie at the café during the thunderstorm. She had missed a week of work without any notification, and Ravi wondered if she was okay. Randy went up to him as he was placing boxes of sugar on a shelf. They weren't supposed to go into that aisle, but Randy didn't say anything—he still felt bad for choking Ravi.

"Just thought I'd let you know that I talked to Annie's mom," Randy said. "She's good, but she went to New York."

"Did anything happen?"

"No, no. Her mother sounded happy. Pleased. She said she needed it. Just needed to get away, I guess. Just thought I'd let you know."

Ravi was glad that Annie left when she needed to. She acted when she knew she needed a change. She couldn't take it anymore. Stimulus. Variety. Her head was about to explode, and she decided to keep it intact instead.

He, in turn, never thought about reacting. He could easily travel around the world. Get out of here. Leave. Go to Paris, London, Cairo, and Moscow. Sleep on the beaches in Greece, with a carton of Bluebell's mint chocolate chip ice cream. Ravi didn't do any of this. He felt his stomach churning as Randy walked away. He didn't have any other friends or even another person he would like to talk to at work. He thought about the noose in his room and the sun setting; he swung back and forth in Ghost Town. He felt like crying, but no tears came from his eyes. He just rubbed them instead. In the middle of Aisle N, he stood with a can of noodle soup in his hand, with the murmur of the store's nightlife tingling in the background, and Ravi felt lost.

Randy gave him the rest of the night off. He felt bad for Ravi. But Ravi didn't want to leave his shift, because he didn't know what else to do. He clocked out and went back to his apartment to brush his teeth. From there he walked to the downtown area. Vavi was nowhere to be seen, so he went to a bar. He hadn't been to one in years—not since his first year in college. He stayed away from these places because he didn't like talking with people too much, nor did he like to drink too much. This bar was a trendy one, and he was surprised that the man at the door let him in. Everyone looked the same as Ravi who was wearing black pants from work, green tennis shoes, and a white undershirt. He walked to the corner of the bar where no one was sitting and ordered a drink. The music was loud, and it made him want to implode—all he could hear was the thunderous bass and a voice whispering in the background. It sounded kind of haunting to him. Some people were dancing to it while others casually shook their heads and moved their lips to the lyrics. A dancing couple stumbled to where Ravi was sitting and began to kiss. They had their hands all over each other. Their tongues were in each other's mouths. The man slipped, taking his friend down with him, and he spilled his beer on Ravi's shirt. Ravi didn't move, nor did he say anything. They got back up and stumbled back to the dance floor. He felt a tap on his shoulder and turned around, thinking for some reason that he was about to get into a fight.

"Here," she said. "Let me help you."

She had a napkin in her hand, and she dabbed his shirt with it. Her tanned face and blue eyeshadow accented her brown eyes. He didn't look at her lips, but at her chin, which was small and rounded just like her earlobes. He wanted to kiss both. She had blond hair, and she was wearing a pink skirt, a black sleeveless top, and a pair of high heels. Her smell—it wasn't a perfume scent, but more of a body lotion of some sort. It was like she just walked out of the shower after cleaning herself with strawberry body wash and shampoo. It was refreshing from the smell of stale beer and smoke wavering through the bar. She dabbed his shirt for a few seconds.

"Thanks," Ravi said. "I'm fine."

"You should have said something," she said. "Otherwise, they'll never learn."

"It's not that easy to learn when you're drunk," Ravi replied. "Besides, I'm not much of a fighter."

"But a lover?" she asked.

"Not much of that either."

"Well," she said. "Take this for the time being."

She handed a small pink coat to him.

"It'll cover up the stain."

"I'm fine," he said. "But thanks, though."

"Take it," she replied. "I don't need it. I don't think I want it anymore. Besides, it'll look good on you."

Ravi put the coat on. The bottom of it came to the middle of his stomach, and the sleeves ended around his forearms.

"Looks a little short," he said.

"Not at all. That's how it's supposed to be worn. Pink looks good on you."

She laughed and sipped her drink. He lit a cigarette. He figured that she would leave and go back to her friends or dance or do whatever she was doing before she was gently dabbing his shirt, but she continued to sit on the barstool next to him. After the pink coat and the beer stain became a faded topic of conversation, they didn't talk to each other for two or three minutes. They both looked around the dance floor. She slightly rocked her head back and forth to the music and smiled. He wanted to ask her to dance. He finished his drink and took off the coat.

"I'm Brandi," she said. "Forgot to introduce myself earlier."

"Hi, Brandi."

"Okay, so what's your name? You're not too good at this are you?"

She laughed.

"Ravi," he said. "Sorry."

"So nice to meet you, Ravi."

"Well," he said. "I'm off."

"You're done already? You're no fun."

She didn't take the coat from his hand.

"Keep it," she said. "It looks nice on you."

Ravi insisted on giving it back to her, but she refused as much as he insisted and gently pushed his hand away.

"I'll tell you what," she said. "I need to sober up. Let's go get some coffee across the street, and then I'll take the coat back."

Ravi didn't want to go out for coffee with her. He didn't feel comfortable in those kinds of situations, where he had to talk to someone sitting directly in front of him, especially a stranger, and especially an attractive stranger. He'd been on two dates, and he had never been in a close relationship. The closest thing was Annie. He would become too nervous, and his mind would stray off to other matters. During the two dates that he had been on, he became uninterested in the other person and started to think about dinosaurs. He would think about how neat it would be to see dinosaurs walking alongside the road, but they weren't mean or vicious or anything. They just kept to themselves, walked along the highways, and drank water from Puget Sound. Every now and then, they would allow children to get on their backs, and they'd give the kids a ride around the city.

"I think I should be getting home," Ravi said.

"Oh, come on," she replied. "Just for a few minutes. I'm not too drunk, just one cup to give me some time to sober up."

She made him put on the coat again. She grabbed his hand and led him out of the bar, but before they left, they stopped in the middle of the dance floor. She moved her hips in a circular motion, like a belly dancer or a charmed snake, and he stood in place as she danced around him. She crouched down, stood up, crouched down again, and traced her hands along his thighs while she oscillated. He looked around the bar, and they were the center of attention as people clapped and shouted at them. Ravi didn't know what else to do, so he just stood and let her press her body against his. He tried hard not to let her notice, but she grinned as the front of his pants puffed out.

"Sorry about that," she said. "I had to get that out of me. I haven't danced all night."

She grabbed his hand again and went outside, not waiting for any of the cars to stop, and they stubbornly walked across the street. Ravi liked how she was holding his hand—it felt natural like their hands should be touching like they'd been holding hands for years. They didn't speak to each other until they got to the coffee shop and sat at a table. She smiled and looked at him. He turned his head away and looked around the room. Not too many other people were there which made him more anxious. He couldn't divert his attention to the random activities of other people.

"I come here a lot after I go out," she said. "It's a nice, quiet place."

"Never been here before."

She appeared to be just as nervous as Ravi. One hand twirled her blond hair, while she tapped her other hand against the table. The waiter came, and they ordered two cups of coffee.

"So why so down?" she asked. "Broke up with your girlfriend?"

"No. Just tired, I guess."

"You know," she said, "I like the ceiling fans here. They're quiet, swift, and they don't make it too cold in here."

"Yeah, they're pretty nice."

"You're not too much of a talker," she said.

He looked up at the fans, and she was right—they circulated just enough air to make it comfortable in the room. The waiter brought the coffee and asked them if they needed anything. Ravi shook his head, but she asked for a plate of pecan pie.

"I have a horrible hunger for sugar," she said. "But I've never had any cavities. I floss almost three or four times a day."

"Wow," Ravi said. "I rarely floss."

"Have you had cavities?" she asked.

"Are you a dentist?"

"I'm a college dropout. Didn't like it. Decided to go another route. I work waiting tables at Caravaggio's—it's an Italian restaurant—to support myself while I paint."

Ravi nodded his head and pulled out a cigarette.

"So, you're a painter?"

"Trying to be," she said. "I haven't shown anything or anything like that. Not quite ready for that yet. But maybe one day."

"I don't know too much about painting."

She sipped her coffee, slowly, breathing in the scent of beans as she closed her eyes.

"Love it," she said. "So, what about you? Where are you from?"

"Indian. My family is from India—Kolkata, but I've lived here all my life. My parents moved here in the 70s for college. Father is an architect, and Mother is a doctor."

The waiter came back with the plate of pecan pie. She thanked him and unwrapped the napkin from the knife and fork. She asked Ravi if he would like a piece, and he declined.

"Interesting," she said, in between bites. "I have an Indian friend from high school. I would go to her house all the time, and all their food—so good and spicy."

She sipped her coffee and took another bite—all in one motion. Ravi was amazed by her ability to eat and talk at the same time—so quickly and efficiently.

"I love those potato samosas. Love them. So weird, my friend, Shivali is her name, she calls her parents Father and Mother, too. I like that. Different from Mom and Dad. Something more touching about it, I think."

Ravi looked around the room, distracted by the sounds of the espresso machines.

"One time I called my parents Mother and Father, and they gave me the oddest look. I never said it again. Funny."

She asked him to tell her more about his family, but he didn't feel like taking the time to tell her about his history, and he just briefly mentioned that he had an older brother. He was sure he wouldn't see her again, he thought, so it didn't matter what he told her.

Ravi put his hand on his knee to make it stop shaking. It had become a nuisance as it caused the table to rattle every time his knee hit the bottom of it.

"What about you?" Ravi asked. "What's your story? Mine is boring."

Her family was from Seattle. She had an older sister, Emily, who lived in New York and was a state lawyer, defending the public. Her parents were both lawyers, as well. She wanted to eventually move to New York and be with her sister while she worked on her art. Her family was close, especially the relationship between the two sisters. She took out her purse and showed Ravi pictures of them. They all looked dignified. The father wore a gray suit and red tie, and his gray hair was neatly combed to the side. His chest was held high, and he had a genuine smile, with his mouth slightly opened. The mother wore a gray suit, as well. No wrinkles were on her face—her skin looked tight against her skeletal structure. She wore a small chain around her neck, and the ring on her finger revealed that the two must be successful lawyers. Emily, the sister, was taller, and her neck was much longer, but the sisters looked alike.

"That's my family," she said. "I love them."

He nodded.

"But, you know," she said, wiping her face with a napkin, "my parents don't really like the route I'm taking. They'd rather me go into law or medicine. I mean, we used to get in these intense arguments that would last for days, but eventually, they gave in."

"Do they still not like the idea?"

"Well, I can tell they're still kind of bitter about it. I don't know, I think they think I'm going to give up one day and go back to school eventually."

Ravi didn't say anything and stared at her face. She moved her head back and forth in a wavelike motion, swirling her head in circles from time to time.

"Do you like to read?" she asked.

She looked at Ravi like she wanted him to say yes— large, glassy round eyes and arched eyebrows.

"Not too much. I never really got into it."

He lied. He used to read all the time—book after book after book—and he would lose himself in these worlds, but soon enough, these worlds became too much like reality, and he had nowhere to escape. From time to time, he would pick up a book, though.

"But I have to say my all-time favorite ending is the end of *All Quiet on the Western Front*," Ravi said.

"I vaguely remember that one," she said. "I think we had to read that for summer reading for, like, seventh or eighth grade."

"Right. That's probably the last time I fully read a book. Remember the ending? I would just read the ending all the time."

She nodded.

"It's the best. The main guy—well, he dies at the end, but he dies with, like, a smile on his face. Like he's happy that it's all over, you know? He's at peace, and even though he's dead, he realizes it's all over. He can relax. It's surreal."

There were a few seconds of silence. She continued to twirl her hair as she finished her pie.

"You're a loner, aren't you?" she asked.

Ravi didn't respond and looked around the room. She laughed.

"Yes. Yes, you are. You were at the bar by yourself, and you weren't even looking to meet up with someone, right? Little did you know that you would meet me."

She laughed again.

"Loners are depressing," she said. "I could never do that. I like having people around. Who wants to live their life alone?"

"Well, it's not as simple as that," Ravi said. "It's not so much wanting to be alone, but more of not wanting to be around people."

Ravi knew that he wasn't making any sense. She kept silent, looking like she was thinking about something.

"But what about love? Sex? Holding hands and going ice skating, or having a picnic at the park and all that stuff? You know we were meant to love, right? Sex and chemistry—it's all in us."

She started talking about matters Ravi didn't feel like talking about. Love, sex—these things were not even dreams to him. He couldn't think about these things when his mind was constantly occupied with hanging himself or thinking about Vavi living on a sidewalk or thinking about the crushed skulls of his parents. Everything he loved was either dead or decaying. If he could get past these images, perhaps he could love, but it meant nothing to him now. She was right—he was a loner. Even in his thoughts, he was alone.

"That's why we're here, right? To love, to have sex, and to live happily, right? Everything else is just a distraction, right?"

"I've never really thought about it," Ravi replied. "I'm just too busy with other things, I guess—like making it through the day. Or not."

She smirked and finished the last bite of pie. Ravi thought about Annie and wondered how she was doing in New York. He hoped she was stepping toward that world of happiness with her trip. Who knows, maybe she had already found a close companion.

"You make it sound so simple," Ravi said.

"I mean, it's not that easy, of course. I've had so many jerk boyfriends. None of them ever really treated me right."

She sat back in her chair.

"It just always takes me a while to realize this. But I'm changing. I'm through with all that. I'm going to find the nice guy, one who treats me right, and have sex all day with him."

She was a talker. He couldn't remember the last time he had heard someone talk so much and so fast and still pay attention. He liked it—he was interested.

"So, what? You're a virgin, right?" Brandi asked.

His heart started to beat faster. He wasn't embarrassed,

he just didn't expect her to ask such a direct question, especially when they barely knew each other. Ravi didn't look at her. He took out his wallet and placed a few dollar bills on the table for the coffee and pie. She looked at him and smiled.

"You don't have to do that," she said. "I'll pay for it."

"It's no problem."

She started singing some song that was playing earlier at the bar.

"Guess I'll go now," Ravi said.

"Yeah, me too. But just one more thing. I don't live too far from here. Do you mind walking me home, so I don't have to walk alone?"

He told her that it wouldn't be a problem at all, despite not wanting to walk her to her house, but she was right— she didn't live too far from the coffee shop, just a couple of blocks. As they approached her door, he walked slowly and let her go ahead. He didn't want to go all the way up to the door with her. She turned around, and he thought she understood his hint, but she grabbed his hand and pulled him toward her, hugged him, and kissed him on the cheek.

"You are a sweetheart, you know?"

Her red door was lit under the porch light. A rocking chair and a small plastic table were on the porch, and a basket full of magazines was next to her door. Brandi took a piece of paper out of her purse and wrote her number on it, and Ravi gave her his contact information. He didn't want to, but he would have felt bad if he didn't after she had given him her number. He hesitated and thought about giving her the incorrect information.

"You made a deal," Ravi said, taking off the pink coat that she gave him.

"You're right, but keep it anyway. It looks good on you."

She handed him the piece of paper.

"No pressure or anything," she said. "But give me a call one day if you want to do something."

"Thanks."

Brandi hugged him again, and Ravi was becoming addicted to her touch. Her strawberry-scented body lotion made him want to kiss her, but he just leaned in, letting her hug him. He kept his hands by his side.

"You want to come in and watch some TV?"

"No thanks," Ravi said.

She waved to him as she walked inside her house. Ravi waved back and put on his new pink coat as he walked away. He did have a fun time at the end of it all—he didn't think about dinosaurs strolling around on the sidewalk.

As Ravi walked away, he thought about his nightly visits to Vavi's bedroom when they were younger. After one of his high school basketball games, his family went out for pizza. Vavi, as usual, was quiet. Father was, too, as he was angry with Ravi because his report card had come in that day, reading a series of C's and one D next to his classes. This was in seventh grade, and his teachers' comments all said the same thing: "Ravi is resting on his laurels. He has so much potential." He didn't know what laurels meant at the time, and he still didn't know what the word meant. Mother tried to break the tension at the table by talking about the basketball game, but they weren't too responsive. Ravi felt so ashamed of his father's anger with him, he didn't want to be there. He didn't want to be anywhere. This was the first time he was ever seriously mad at Ravi—so mad that he kept silent and avoided looking at his son. Father was a disciplined man who liked to have fun—who was fun—but when it came down to studying, he was strict. He never had to worry about Vavi because Vavi always made straight A's. Ravi could feel Father's disgust for him with every loud breath Father made while biting into his jalapeño-filled pizza slice. Ravi remembered how he had kept looking at Vavi, but he never made eye contact with him, either, as his brother silently chewed his pizza and sipped his iced tea. Mother ran her hand through Ravi's hair and tried to make conversation with him, and Ravi felt bad because he wanted to respond. He wanted her to be able to enjoy the night, but he just couldn't do anything. Father finally broke the silence.

"No more anything," he said. "No TV. No going out. No more playing sports with Vavi every day. You will study, every day, and bring your grades up. Take pride in knowledge."

"Can I at least play basketball with Vavi on the weekends?"

"No," Father said. "Not until you get better grades."

Mother kept silent, though Ravi could tell she wanted to say something, they all knew that saying anything would just worsen the situation.

"How about on Sundays for a couple of hours?" Vavi asked.

"I said no."

"But think about it," Vavi said. "Physical activity is just as important as mental. It's a balance. The body needs it. You of all people should know this."

Father looked at him as he wiped his mouth with a napkin. His eyes opened slightly, and perspiration made its way down from his hair to his forehead because of the peppers he was eating.

"Okay. That's fine."

Father looked at Ravi.

"Take your studies seriously. It's for your future."

His voice was still stern, not easing up. Mother put her hand on Ravi's arm, still not saying anything.

Later on that night, Ravi went into Vavi's room. As

always, he was in bed with a book in his hand, but this time he didn't bother hiding the Vodka—it was on top of the covers, leaning against his thigh.

"Aren't you worried that they'll walk in?" Ravi asked.

"They're sleeping," he said.

He took a sip.

"Don't ever let me catch you doing this," he said. "My anger at you will be worse than Father's."

He was drunk. Vavi was the first drunk person Ravi had ever seen. He had only heard about it or seen it on television, but there before him was his brother, half gone.

"Don't you think you've been drinking too much?" Ravi asked.

Vavi told him to stop asking him questions, and they remained silent.

Ravi remembered looking around his room, though he'd been in there a million times. It was the kind of looking around he did when he was in someone's house for the first time, not knowing what to say. That was the first time Ravi felt awkward being around his brother.

On the way back to his apartment from Brandi's house, Ravi saw Vavi was back in his spot outside the coffee shop. He was writing, talking to himself as he worked. Ravi sat down next to him.

"So, there's this huge, slimy, jellyfish. Horrific to humans. It's transparent and engulfs everything, and everything it eats can be seen through the outer layer of the creature's skin or whatever. It has these tentacles, numbing."

He closed his eyes, his eyebrows lifted to the top of his forehead, and his cheeks dented inwards. His head propped against the café wall. He was in a trance—a drunken daze. His eyes opened, and Ravi looked straight into his enlarged pupils, half covered by his eyelids and surrounded by red veins, and listened, as this could be the only time Vavi talked about his script to Ravi.

"And all the people who have been swallowed can be seen by their loved ones, and I'm not sure if any of the ingested will die. Maybe at the end, when the jellyfish is defeated, they can go back to their friends and family, covered in glop. I guess the thing won't be exactly biologically correct, but it's also a gigantic monster which allows it to be biologically unnatural."

Ravi felt his eyebrows lower as he listened intently. Vavi loved science-fiction movies, especially the bad B-rated kinds—the ones where the microphone could be seen hanging over the actors, or when some of the stage crew could be heard talking in the background. This sounded like an homage to his favorite kind of movie.

"Buildings, too," Vavi mumbled. "It will swallow whole buildings and monuments, and they'll all float inside of it. There goes the Eiffel Tower, the Washington Monument, and the Taj Mahal. And there won't be any crime going on, because everyone will be worried about the jellyfish. Everyone unites to fight the jellyfish and not each other."

He smiled.

"Move in with me."

"Do we have to go through this again?"

"Just move in with me. I don't understand why you won't."

"Look. I'm happy. I like this life. If I get tired of it, then maybe I will. I will get a job. I will find a place to move. But I don't need any of that right now."

"Move in with me."

"It's not that easy," he said. "I can't just move in like that. And you know that, too. Just let it go. You're happy, right? Things are good for you, right? You have a job. You have your own place to stay. And whatever happened with that girl you liked?"

No answer. The streets were empty now. The neon lights were on their last blinks. The bus stops were surrounded by litter from throughout the day, and the smell of the beer on Ravi's shirt settled in, making him want to take off all his clothes. Vavi asked him about his pink jacket. Ravi didn't answer. Vavi put his arm around his shoulder. Ravi thought that maybe it was not the smell of beer on his shirt, but the stench of downtown on Vavi that made him feel like throwing up. He wanted to tell Vavi about his dreams. He wanted to talk to him about their parents, but he didn't speak. Maybe if he happened to catch him sober one day.

"You need to move on," Vavi continued. "You need to open up, have a relationship, be happy. I don't know, maybe move away. Move on. Experience things instead of just locking yourself up in your own head."

"Well, what about you? You're not doing anything."

"Don't worry about me," Vavi replied.

His eyes narrowed, and his brows shifted, pointing toward his eyes.

"I chose this life. I'm happy. Content. You? You didn't choose your life. You're living like a zombie. Do something. I think of you, and I think about how you can do so much, but you live a lonely life, shunning the world. Why?"

Vavi and Ravi had never spoken about their parents' deaths before, and Ravi wished that Vavi knew his reasoning. That he hid from the world because his parents were gone and because his brother was slowly losing himself to his life on the streets. Could one live as if nothing had happened? Vavi had to have known this. Why did he ignore that? Had Vavi moved on? Ravi lost his patience.

"I think of you, and I see a mind that has been eroded and decayed. A scared mind."

He tapped his fingers against the sidewalk.

"You don't choose to live this life—you just hate reality. You're scared. Scared just as much as I am, but you won't admit it."

"There's nothing to admit," Vavi replied.

"Come on, Vavi. You were the best student in your class. All kinds of offices were calling you for jobs, but you didn't do anything. What did you do? You sleep next to trash cans smelling of vomited beer."

"Shut up," Vavi said. "Shut the fuck up."

Ravi had gotten to him. At least that was something. Some kind of reaction. Now Ravi wanted to see how far he could go. Vavi stood up and leaned against the wall as he wobbled back and forth.

"Do you even know Mother and Father died?" Ravi continued. "It's like you can't care less that their heads were fucking bashed in with baseball bats. You saw their bodies."

Ravi raised his voice, almost shouting, standing up at the same time. He felt like he was trying to learn a foreign language when he cursed.

"You saw their heads all mashed against the wall, with their fucking blood and brains spread everywhere."

Vavi clenched both hands into fists. Ravi closed his eyes while he waited for a punch, but Vavi remained still. His voice remained calm but stern, like Father's. Ravi opened his eyes.

"That was almost seven years ago," Vavi said. "You can't still be getting over that or you'll never live like you're supposed to. What? You want to live like this the rest of your life?"

He shook his head. The city was quiet—twirling, but it was quiet.

"What's the point of living, then, if you don't know how to live?" Vavi continued. "If you don't want to live? Do something. Stop living like you're dead."

He stamped his feet and clapped his hands.

"There are too many of those in the world. Show people what it's like to move on. Show them a reason to live—why you live."

Ravi wanted to believe him, but he was being a hypocrite.

"Well, what the fuck? They die and you become homeless. What am I supposed to think about that? The guy I look up to the most is giving up."

Ravi paced in short circles.

"I never gave up. I'm still going. I'm serious about this manuscript. This is just a sabbatical. Like I've gone to France to teach there for a few years."

Vavi rubbed his forehead and the back of his neck.

"I'm going to come back. Don't worry about me—I'm okay. It's you."

Ravi knew, then, that Vavi still remembered. He did. He was half gone, but he still remembered.

10

He was back at the apartment. He was hanging again. This time his vision went back and forth between being in Ghost Town and seeing Brandi at a coffee shop—it was a different café from the one they had gone to, and they looked like they were good friends as they talked, laughed, and smiled. He didn't know what they were talking about, because everything was muted, and then he saw himself hanging again in Ghost Town. Everything was the same. It was in the evening, and the cowboy hat and the rope were there. Then the reverie switched back to Brandi. Then the reverie went back to Ravi hanging again. He squinted his eyes to see if he could recognize anything else in the cowboy setting and to see if his own eyes were open, or if his stomach was moving to show that he was still alive, but he couldn't see anything.

Then he thought about when he and Vavi would play Pick-up Sticks. Ravi was good at the game, better than his brother. Vavi would marvel at his steady hands and his precise movements of the plastic sticks. It was the only game that Vavi didn't have to try to lose to make his brother happy. "Steady, steady," Ravi would whisper as he would try to remove a stick. And once he succeeded, he would sigh and look at his brother with a smile and see his brother smiling back at him.

"Steady," Ravi said, as he stared at the ceiling in his bedroom.

Ravi wished his brother was there with him at the apartment. He wished Vavi was around so he could tell him about Brandi. He thought about Brandi. Now that they weren't around each other, and because he wasn't nervous anymore, he liked her. She was vibrant and fun, and she reminded him of a sunflower.

He didn't bother trying to sleep and decided to go for a walk along Broadway—he wore the pink coat. It was late, and most of the people on the street didn't look too comforting. Traffic lights were the only things illuminating the streets. There were small groups of people on each corner of each block. As he waited for the pedestrian light to switch, a man told Ravi that he would give him a quarter for a cigarette.

"Here," Ravi said. "Just take one. Keep your quarter."

"Nice coat," the man replied.

Ravi didn't understand. He didn't understand the purpose of life, and the reasons for interaction. Why must we have others be happy? He guessed that scientists had a biological or chemical explanation for this, and religious people had spiritual answers. Why must we be around others? The people who Ravi wanted to be around had left— his parents were dead, and his brother was homeless. These were the most important people to him, and he couldn't be with them.

Ravi wanted to see Brandi smile or hear her laugh. He wanted to ask her the questions that he had been asking himself. Or they didn't even have to talk to each other—just being around her in silence would be nice. The world seemed too surreal and maybe too unreal. Reality. One of the greatest philosophical questions is—what is reality? Was he hanging in Ghost Town, or was he walking down Broadway? Ravi didn't feel alive in either world.

"I think, therefore, I'm dead," he said to himself.

Why must people feel lonely? He wished everyone could all be self-sufficient and only depend on their own bodies and minds because then a lot of hurt would be erased. The homeless people he walked by wouldn't feel lonely. Annie wouldn't feel lonely. Depression would more likely decrease, along with suicide rates. He didn't know too much about philosophy, and this was probably the extent of his deep thoughts, but he did believe that if you were mentally weak and you didn't have much going for you, it was really hard to keep going. It was a lot easier to stay in bed. It was a lot easier to hang yourself.

Ravi remembered when Vavi was maddest with him during an incident that occurred while they played baseball on the street. They played with some of their neighbors with a tennis ball, and big rocks were used as bases. Two unknown boys came to their street, cursed at them, and took their tennis ball. They ran off, and Vavi and his brother, and his friends started to chase them. Ravi was nine at the time, and he didn't know what was going on, but he decided to run with them—he thought they had just started a new kind of game. After several minutes of running, the group turned a corner, and Ravi saw the two guys standing in the middle of a crowd of boys. Once his brother and his friends saw this large gang, they turned around and ran in the other direction. The gang began to chase Vavi's group of friends. Ravi still didn't know what was going on, but he turned around and ran, as well. He was the youngest of his baseball companions, and he was a little slower than the rest of them. He finally became too tired to run at his fastest speed and slowed down considerably. Ravi looked at his brother and admired his strength as he was at the head of the pack. Vavi turned around, saw Ravi jogging, and ran back to him.

"Ravi, hurry up. Hurry up. Run faster."

"I'm tired."

"Ravi, they're going to beat us up. You've got to run faster."

"But I can't."

"Ravi, hurry the fuck up."

That was the first time he had heard Vavi curse. He had never seen such anger in his brother's eyes before, and he had never heard his brother speak in such a low, harsh voice. It was then that Ravi realized that they weren't playing a new game, but that they were in a dangerous situation. Vavi grabbed his brother's hand, and Ravi was forced to run faster to keep up with him, or else Ravi would have been dragged. The brothers ran into a neighbor's yard and hid in a shed. They waited in the dark for ten minutes, breathing hard, and they never saw the group of guys who were chasing them.

"I'm sorry for cursing, Ravi. We needed to go, though, otherwise who knows what would have happened? I'm not too good of a fighter, you know."

"I understand."

He didn't understand. He didn't understand why they were in danger, but he was glad that everyone was okay. Vavi hugged him in the dark, and they went home for dinner.

Ravi realized later that, though it appeared Vavi was angry with him, it was not so much that he was mad at his younger brother—Vavi just wanted to protect him. Ravi believed that if Vavi didn't run back to fetch him, he probably would have stopped on the sidewalk, and the group of guys would have caught up to him. As he walked along Broadway, he thought about how badly he wanted to be in that shed with his brother, exiling themselves from the rest of the world.

11

"So, what's been going on?" Brandi asked. "I've called you a couple of times and I never heard back. I didn't think you'd come to meet me."

They were at Pike Place Market, walking past the stores. People were everywhere—tourists, natives, the homeless, Brandi, and Ravi. The smell of fish hovered around, a thick scent, making Ravi feel like he was swimming in it. He felt nauseous, and he breathed through his mouth as much as possible. The sun came in, giving a dreamlike aura to the place. He felt like he was on a postcard. In certain spots, where the sun's beams were strong, he could see the dust particles wavering around in the air like flies. Everyone looked happy, buying their food or clothes, feeding the pigeons, or just walking around.

"Not much," Ravi said.

"Nothing? I thought you may have been busy or something."

"Not really."

Sighing, she stopped at a souvenir store and looked at a stand of license plates that had various names inscribed on them. She found one with Brandi on it.

"Look to see if they have my name," Ravi said.

"Yeah, right. You want to get some crepes?"

"I'll watch you eat, but I won't get anything. I don't have much of an appetite right now."

"What's wrong?"

"Nothing."

"Did you already eat?"

"Not too long ago."

It had been about a day.

Brandi ordered a chocolate and strawberry crepe, and they stood at the counter as he watched her eat. Ravi was obsessed with looking around, seeing everything, and observing everyone else. He saw long noses, huge stomachs, or the strands of hair that covered balding men's heads. He saw the old woman who sat on the red bench, talking to herself, and the children who stared at her like she was a part of a zoo. A woman wearing a blue skirt, sunglasses, and long black high heels clicked and clacked her way around, calling someone's name. Maybe it was her husband or child. It was all dizzying—too much going on at the same time. Brandi sighed again and took a small bite out of her crepe.

"I used to come here a lot with my family," Brandi said. "We would get crepes every week. And sometimes we would go to the harbor and take a boat tour and look at all the buildings. It's pretty, especially on a day like this."

"I can't remember the last time I've been here," Ravi said. "Maybe not since high school—I'm not sure."

"For a guy who has a lot of time on his hands, you sure don't do much."

"Do you want a balloon?" Ravi asked.

He took off and came back with a red balloon that read, "Happy Birthday."

"It's not my birthday," Brandi said.

"It's always your birthday."

Brandi went to the restroom before they went for a walk along the harbor. As he waited, Ravi felt the colors of his surroundings—the blues, reds, yellows, skirts, pants, fish, pizza, laughing, shouting, the children, and pigeons—all crashing down on him. He wanted to be in his bed. He wanted to be sleeping between his parents as he had when he was a child. Ravi closed his eyes, hoping to release this overwhelming pressure of brightness—of life. He opened his eyes. She held his hand.

They listened to the world around drown from the sounds of the water and the horns of the docking ships. Seagulls swooped up and down like they were in the ballet. Brandi squeezed his hand tighter like she couldn't stand without him. Ravi looked at her eyes and saw light red creeping in from the sides, making its way to the pupils. She wasn't herself. A grin crept in as the drug made its way through her blood, and she leaned on Ravi's shoulder as they walked. Brandi tried hard not to let him notice, but it was harder for Ravi not to realize that she had taken something in the restroom. They stopped walking, and Brandi lifted her face toward the sun and closed her eyes, letting the light take her away. Ravi did the same.

He bought her an ice cream cone—mint chocolate chip in a small waffle cone. They talked about the people around them, giving them names, and making up stories about them. Ravi was amazed at how observant Brandi could be, talking about the patterns on the wooden boards of the harbor, those natural swirls found in the wood, and how they reminded her of Munch's *The Scream*. In the sunlight, with her red eyes and flip-flops, Ravi realized that Brandi was lost, though she tried not to reveal it. She was just as lost as he was—not sure what life was all about. She wanted to escape just as much as he wanted to escape.

"You want to come over for dinner tonight?" Brandi asked. "Family dinner. Going over to my parents' house."

He pretended to think about it for a bit.

"I'd rather not."

"Come on," she said. "There's food. Both my parents are great cooks. Tasty food."

She wrote down her parents' address in big bubble letters where the dots for the i's were circles rather than dots.

"Come meet me around seven tonight," Brandi said.

"I guess."

"Do you want a ride right now? To your apartment?"

"I'm okay. I'll walk."

"Whatever. I'll see you tonight."

12

Her parents' house was huge. As Ravi took a tour, he saw that it was a four-bedroom house on the bottom, with a guestroom and a bathroom on the second floor. Her mother, Mrs. Sanders, wore a gray skirt with a matching jacket, as she had just come home from the office. Like Brandi, she had blond hair, but it looked dyed, as the roots revealed a mixture of brown and gray. She had small wrinkles around her eyes, and her face looked rubbery and shiny, covered in cosmetics and skin cream. The house smelled of roasted chicken and corn. Brandi's father sat in the living room, reading the newspaper while sipping a beer. Brandi was in the shower. Ravi felt guilty for eating dinner with her family while all this time Auntie had been trying to get him to go over to her house.

Mrs. Sanders asked Ravi if he would like something to drink. Her smile was unforced, full of natural pleasure. He told her no thanks and sat in the living room with Mr. Sanders while Mrs. Sanders finished setting the table. Ravi asked her if she needed any help, but she was whistling so loud, that she didn't hear him.

Mr. Sanders was reading *Newsweek*, and Ravi snuck glances at him, noticing his thin frame, contrasting his square jaw and pointed nose. His narrow black eyes were almost hidden by his jutting cheekbones.

Ravi looked around the room and noticed how there were pictures everywhere—on every shelf, coffee table, and wall space. He got up and looked at them. Mr. Sanders said something, but Ravi didn't hear him, as his mind wandered off into the worlds found between frames. Most of the pictures were of Brandi and her sister when they were younger. Ravi was surprised to see that several of them were of Brandi dressed in a cheerleading outfit—blue and white. Another photo showed her with her family at the beach, underneath a large blue umbrella. They were all wearing sunglasses and eating sandwiches. Brandi's father had a well-defined stomach, and her mother was just as attractive as the sisters in her red bikini, revealing slender legs doused in the sand. Looking at those pictures of Brandi, Ravi would have never connected the two, from back then and now. In another frame, she was at a high school dance, surrounded by her girlfriends, wearing a long white dress, her hair fixed in a beehive shape. He stared at the face and pictured her face now and thought about how dark she had become. Not darker like skin color, but darker by the vibes she gave off. He would have never pictured her becoming an artist, surrounding herself with people wearing black shirts all the time, talking about how the world was so fucked up.

"I guess you didn't know Brandi back then," Mr. Sanders said.

"No, not back then. She looks so different."

"She was a sweetie back then. Well, she's still a sweetheart, but things were different back then. I guess you know how it goes with your parents."

"Right."

Brandi came downstairs, hair still wet from the shower and smelling of peach body lotion.

"Oh no," she said. "Don't look at those."

"Could you do a routine for me?" Ravi asked.

"Shut up."

She grabbed Ravi's hand and led him to the dining room. Mr. Sanders looked at Ravi up and down.

"Well, you look nice," he said.

Pink coat and torn jeans.

"Sorry," Ravi said. "Didn't have time to change."

"No really, I like the coat. It's different, but it looks good on you."

"I said the same thing, Daddy," Brandi said.

Daddy. *That must be a glimpse into the past*, Ravi thought. *When he would come home after work and Brandi was a little girl, running to him to hug him, calling him Daddy.*

They talked and asked Ravi questions, and he nodded or shook his head. He answered with "yes, sir," or "no, ma'am." He had never addressed anyone like that before, not even his parents, except when they were mad at him. Was he trying to impress them? He kept his knee shaking to a minimum, and when it started to rattle the table, Brandi put her hand on his thigh to calm him down. Ravi wanted to lick those fingers pressed on his lap and felt guilty about this urge, as her parents were sitting directly across from him. They went through all the usual questions. What did he do for a living? Where did he go to school? Did he have any siblings? What did he think about the weather? Though they were uninteresting questions, Ravi was glad that they stuck with the standard ones. They asked about his parents, and Ravi didn't say much, not telling them about his parents' death, but just talking about their professions and how they came to America. The Sanders were interested in India, and the father talked about taking a trip to Agra one day to see the Taj Mahal. They talked about how they had been all around the world, but they had never made it to India. Mrs. Sanders said she liked to cook Indian food, but she was no good at it, and she mentioned that maybe one day Ravi could come over and be one of her taste-testers. Brandi was livelier than earlier that day at Pike's Market, talking in a lighter tone of voice, supporting Ravi as he talked, shaking or nodding her head when he did.

"I'm sure Brandi has told you about her painting," Mr. Sanders said.

"Yeah, she has. That's great."

"Sure, it is."

Ravi could tell Brandi's parents loved their daughter, and that they held a good spirit within themselves, but there was something eerie floating behind them, like when parents have just had an argument before they had company over and they put on these masks to hide any bad vibes. Ravi looked at Brandi. She was chewing away at her roasted chicken and mashed potatoes. Ravi took small bites and tried his best not to be impolite, but he just couldn't eat it. He asked them if he could be excused, and where he could find the washroom.

"Washroom?" Mr. Sanders said.

He laughed loudly, almost choking on his food. Brandi had to hit him on his back.

"The bathroom is just past the living room, on the right," he said.

"Here, let me show you, dear," Mrs. Sanders said.

Ravi put on the vent and ran the faucet while he tried to vomit as quietly as possible. He washed his eyes to get rid of any of the red that came with throwing up. When he got back to the dining room, they were all staring at him. Mrs. Sanders looked like she wanted to say something, but just faintly smiled instead.

"I'm sorry about this," Ravi said. "But I think I should go. I'm not feeling too well, and I haven't been for a couple of days."

Mrs. Sanders asked him if he needed any kind of medicine, and he told her that he had some at his place. Mr. Sanders wiped his face with a dark blue napkin and stood up. Ravi thanked them repeatedly for having him over, and he apologized again for cutting the visit so short. They were more than understanding, asking him to come back again when he felt better.

"Maybe next time you can try some of my Indian cooking," Mrs. Sanders said. "I'm nervous just thinking about it."

"I look forward to it, Mrs. Sanders—thank you so much for dinner. Thank you, Mr. Sanders."

Brandi walked Ravi to the door and stepped outside with him.

"You okay?" she asked.

"Yeah, just not used to eating so much."

"You did well," she said. "I think they like you. Daddy thinks you're weird, I'm sure. But everyone who's not wearing a suit is weird to him."

"Thanks again," Ravi said. "I really did have a fun time."

"Give me a call sometime."

She pecked him on the cheek. He wanted to slide his tongue as far as possible into her mouth.

"Bye," Ravi said.

13

This time he was in the middle of the ocean, beneath the surface of the water, but everything else was still there—the wooden boards un-soaked, the bright white cowboy hat was below his feet, and he was hanging. He wasn't floating—the weight of the water seemed to be pulling him down, and as each wave rolled over, it put more pressure, causing him to choke. And every time he choked, his eyes popped open, but once the wave passed, his eyes closed again. Dolphins and goldfish surrounded him. They looked at him, wondering why he wasn't floating or swimming, staying in one spot. They sniffed him, like dogs, checking to see if he was alive. He tried to lift his hands to pet them, but he couldn't move. A tiger, walking on the ocean surface, stopped and looked at him, and then jumped to him, floating, trying to gnaw the rope to set him free. Nothing happened, and the tiger went back to the floor and chewed seaweeds. At least this time he got some variety.

14

In his apartment, Ravi sat on the couch and thought about when he was younger and his family was in the living room, and they were watching some Bollywood movie on satellite television. Ravi didn't understand Hindi, but his parents were both fluent in Hindi and Bengali. He just sat and watched the ladies dance, moving their hips and necks, carving the air with their arms and hands, like they were floating underneath the surface of a body of water. During one dance scene, Mother stood up and started dancing just like the ladies in the movie. Ravi had never seen her do this, and he was impressed by the control she had—her pitter-pattering feet, the swaying, and curving of her body. Both of the brothers were in shock, their mouths wide open and gasping, when Father got up and started to dance, too. Even on Father's happiest of days, Ravi could never imagine him doing such a thing. Father held Mother's hands as they swung each other around, playing hide and seek and hard to get. Vavi, with a smirk on his face, joined in and started doing his own kind of routine like he was a professional dancer. Ravi got up, too, but he didn't know how to dance, so he just ran and skipped around the coffee table, shouting and laughing.

Ravi thought about his parents when they were younger, living in Kolkata as teenagers—flirting with each other, trying to catch each other's eyes, kissing when no one was looking, sneaking out in the middle of the night to the Ganges, and lighting candles and putting them on lotus flowers and watching them drift off into the darkness.

Despite the strong custom of arranged marriages, theirs wasn't fixed. They fell in love at Albert Hall, a coffee house. She asked him how he liked the book he was reading—Tagore's *A Grain Of Sand*. After their deaths, Ravi had asked Auntie about his parents and how they ended up together, and she said that, when Father was telling her how they met, as soon as Mother with her round watery eyes, bright red lips, and soft black pupils, asked him that question about the book, Father decided that he wanted to be with her. And Mother said that, as soon as she saw Father sitting at the table by himself, reading and smoking a pipe, with his hair oiled and neatly combed to the side, she didn't want to talk to him at all, thinking that he would be a jerk. But when he looked up at her, and she saw the vulnerability hidden behind his stern face, she sighed.

The couple living in the apartment next door were having sex. Ravi heard the guy moaning. He heard her cursing. He put his hand up to the wall and felt their vibrations. They had been living there for at least as long as Ravi had been living here. He didn't talk to them much—mainly just hello, goodbye, and about the weather. Her name was Caroline, and she had blue eyes and shoulder-length black hair. At all times of the day, she looked like a celebrity doing a photo shoot. Sometimes when they ran into each other, she looked at Ravi like she had known him all his life. Her boyfriend was a nice guy. He looked like he worked out all day—rock solid biceps, and horse muscle calves. His name was Eric. Ravi would hear them having sex three times a week, on average.

He didn't feel like listening to them that night, so he got his Walkman from the closet—he hadn't used it in a few years. He replaced the batteries and listened to the Tupac cassette that hadn't left the tape player since he had last used it and looked out the window. This didn't last for too long, and he started to think about Brandi. He kept thinking about how she gave him her jacket and wiped the beer stain on his shirt. Such simple actions, small movements, but this feeling of someone taking care of him, giving him attention, added up to something greater than just those tiny gestures. He turned off the Walkman and went back to the wall and listened to Caroline and Eric having sex. He found himself exploring his own body—something he hadn't done since junior high—and unzipped his pants and pictured Brandi and himself as the couple next door.

15

He saw teenagers standing in line at the corn dog hut as he walked along Broadway at night, feeling the sidewalk's grime squishing against the soles of his shoes. Customers huddled in groups, wearing ski caps, hoodies, and baggy jeans, some with their hands in their pockets. Some stood outside the crowd, while others were in the middle, with arms flailing, cursing, and shouting. They all looked the same to Ravi. On the corner of the block, just under the pedestrian streetlight, sat a homeless man wearing a brown overcoat and black steel-toed boots, sitting cross-legged as he asked the teenagers for money. Some taunted him, instead, dropping ketchup packets into his jar of loose change, and they pulled on the small blanket he sat on, causing him to fall over. But others put coins into the jar or gave him cigarettes. Ravi wondered how many of these teenagers would become homeless. He wondered if they would eventually realize that, despite the world's physical appearance—a hard mahogany brown shell, full of thin pricking needles—inside was a core composed of soft, tender, and juicy bits and pieces of sentiments, memories, and dreams. That underneath the harshness of the outside layer, perhaps hidden, was a place where everyone wanted to be loved.

He continued walking, after dropping a few coins in the jar, and one of the teenagers asked Ravi for a cigarette. Ravi didn't talk or look at him, and the guy cursed at him, calling him a fucking jerk. Ravi thought about turning around. He thought about grabbing him by the neck and pushing him against the side of the restaurant. He almost cared. He kept walking.

The next block was dead, lit by neon signs and traffic lights. There was a Kinkos with one employee in it, tying his shoelaces as he talked on the phone. The air was cold that night, thin and piercing, eroding his skin as the acerbic odor wavered from the trashcans and filled his nostrils. Every few minutes, a car drove by, slowly, blaring rap or rock, windows down, with puffs of smoke shooting out. Sporadically, Ravi saw a few late-night dog walkers window shopping as their pets urinated on the curb. Once they reached the end of the block, they turned around, staying away from the bright lights of the corn dog store. A homeless man mumbled for a cigarette. Ravi gave him a couple, as well as some change.

He continued walking, going up a hill, into a residential area, where the stench subsided, giving way to potpourri-scented gardens. He closed his eyes—his hamstrings tightened, and he heard his breathing grow louder, going deeper, and he counted the three steps it took for him to cover each segment of the sidewalk. Right foot, left foot, then right foot. Left foot, right foot, then left foot. Small strides. Dogs from the backyards barked. He felt—as his walking slowed down, as his body leaned forward more, head almost parallel to the ground—that he was almost at the top. The sidewalk leveled off, and he opened his eyes while turning around.

He saw downtown Seattle before him in layers, like a crumbling wedding cake. Patches of light sparsely glittered the city. Though it was night, he saw gray. The view reminded him of when his old VCR broke. Vavi had opened it up with a screwdriver, dissecting the inside as they had done to frogs in high school Biology class. Vavi had told his brother to look inside, and when he peered over the table he saw black and gray pieces and patterns of plastic and metal. That's what he thought he saw now. Some plastic and metal pieces were taller than others, and there were splotches of green throughout, like looking at fields of grass from an airplane in the sky. As Ravi thought about it, he thought of some depressing, worn-down circus. Clowns full of holes and lions with no teeth. He thought about his life. He whispered Brandi's name over and over.

He stood there for a few minutes before walking to his aunt's house which was on the same street, one block down. He unlatched the gate leading to the backyard and snuck in around one in the morning and sat on a green, wooden lawn chair for a few minutes. The night was quiet in her backyard, exiled from the rest of the world. He started raking the backyard under the moonlight. His heels crunched over vines and broken branches—the wind crawled down his neck, reminding him of Bruce Lee's grave. He took puffs in between scraping soil.

He was surprised that Auntie hadn't woken up from the sound of crackling leaves being gathered in mounds, looking like gophers had raced around and around the yard. Ants picked at his ankles, but he didn't do anything. He let them bite. He let them get what they wanted because he was too busy thinking about fifth grade.

His class took a field trip to Hard Rock Café because they had been behaving well. "Miss American Pie" came on the radio while they ate burgers. Everyone in Ravi's class, plus the teachers and chaperones, knew the song except for him, and they all sang along. They sang it like a national anthem. Ravi kept his mouth closed and looked around while everyone was shouting with their hands on each other's shoulders, swaying back and forth. He felt so out of place that he took two bites out of his cheeseburger, and he remembered wishing that Vavi was there with him and that no one else was around, just the two of them. The teacher, Ms. Sewings, got mad at Ravi for not eating his food, saying that his mother would be angry with him for wasting money, but then her face, which was full of crevices and creases, eased up, and she asked Ravi in a gentle voice if he didn't eat his food because it was against his religion. Ravi nodded his head, lying, and she offered to give him some more money so he could buy another meal. He didn't take her money and asked for Vavi instead.

He listened to the same song again in ninth grade when he found out that it was about the death of Buddy Holly, as well as a couple of other singers. It made him cry, even though he didn't know much about their lives or their music. He still didn't know all of the lyrics, but he sang, "this will be the day that I die" over and over while he made his way around the backyard.

16

The night before their parents' murder, Father caught Vavi smoking in the driveway. Ravi was there, watching his brother inhaling and exhaling, watching the smoke coming out his nostrils and mouth, wondering how it all worked. He let Ravi take a drag, and Ravi almost choked, coughing and gasping for oxygen. Ravi said that he would never smoke again and that he couldn't see why Vavi smoked.

Father was up around two in the morning to get a glass of water when he saw the glowing orange of the cigarette through the window. Vavi didn't throw away the cigarette when Father walked out—at least not immediately—not until Father told him to throw it out. The brothers both went inside and received such a loud scolding that Mother rushed to the living room with large eyes and loud breathing. This was the maddest Ravi had ever seen his father, shouting how disgusted he was with them, calling them idiots, saying how ashamed he was with them. Ravi was relieved that Vavi was able to hide his drunkenness, or else they would have had to hear it for at least another hour. Vavi remained silent the whole time, staring at the ground with his hands in his lap, while Ravi tried to interject now and then, though he knew that Father wouldn't give them a chance to speak. Mother remained silent, as well, but it wasn't the silence Ravi was used to—this silence was filled with disappointment, not sympathy. After Father finished scolding them, he walked back to his bedroom, followed by Mother. The brothers went back to their own rooms, but Ravi couldn't sleep, so he went to see if Vavi was still awake. He was in bed, reading a book on Eastern philosophy while sipping Vodka.

"I've never seen Father so angry," Ravi said.

"Well, he should be," Vavi replied.

He spoke in a quiet voice—not a whisper, but with a calm tone. He didn't seem shaken up at all from the lecture they had just received.

"What do you mean?"

"I mean, he did what he was supposed to do," Vavi said. "He's a good father. He loves us."

He took another sip and told Ravi to go to bed because he wanted to get up early and play outside the next day. This made Ravi happy. It made him think that everything would be okay and that Father would soon forgive them.

The next morning, Father went to Ravi's bedroom. He was still sleeping or just waking up from sleeping, still in dream mode. Father ran his hand through Ravi's hair, and Ravi was glad that he did this, but Ravi turned his back to him. Father knew Ravi was awake, and he told Ravi that he loved him. Ravi never responded. He didn't say anything. For no reason, Ravi was mad at him and gave him the silent treatment. Father kissed him on the cheek and walked out of the room. Mother came in soon after, and Ravi acted the same way, no matter how badly he wanted to cry and tell her how sorry he felt.

17

Brandi had left a note on Ravi's door while he was in Auntie's backyard. *She must have been up late*, Ravi thought, because he didn't leave the apartment until midnight, and he got back around three. He was glad that Brandi was up late. He was glad that Brandi wasn't sleeping, just like himself. They hadn't spoken to each other since dinner at her house one week ago. The note read that she had enjoyed spending time with him, and she wanted to meet up again. She told him to meet her in the S section on the third floor of the library which was open twenty-four hours during the semester.

As Ravi walked inside the library, he was swamped with the smell of musty, old books, causing his eyes to water. The lights were dim, the humming loud, and there weren't too many people inside, but he could hear mumbled chattering as he walked to the stairs. The lady at the help desk was reading a book as Ravi passed by and told him, without looking up, that no food or drinks were allowed.

On the third floor, Ravi walked around the room, looking for the S section, and making his way through the maze. He walked from one end to the other end, finally thinking that Brandi wasn't there or that maybe there wasn't an S section on the third floor. But as he walked to the stairs, he saw someone sitting at a table facing a wall. Ravi looked at the shelves and saw that it was in the S section. He shouted her name. Brandi jumped and turned around.

"You came," she shouted. Her words echoed.

When he got to the table, he saw a stack of large books she had been studying: an anthology of French painters, an anthology of Italian painters, and a couple of books on art theory and technique. Her tangled hair was tied in a bun with loose strands sticking out, making her look like she had just been electrocuted. No makeup. A pimple on her chin. Ravi wanted to kiss the pimple.

"I look like a mess, I know," Brandi said. "Please excuse my appearance."

"You look great," Ravi said, in a high-pitched voice.

He asked her how she had been doing, making sure to talk in a lower tone of voice.

"Not so good," Brandi replied. "Had to work a double today because one of the waiters couldn't make it in."

Her head swayed back and forth like she was about to fall asleep.

"I thought I'd come here and study a bit on painting. I've been meaning to do it forever now, and I was planning on coming here after my morning shift to spend the day here. Looks like I'm going to spend the night here, instead."

"You want some coffee?" Ravi asked.

"No thanks. I've been drinking some all day, plus I took some caffeine pills."

She rubbed her arms and thighs, trying to keep herself warm.

"They keep it so cold in here," Brandi said.

Without thinking, Ravi rubbed her arms.

"Here, take this," he said, taking off the pink coat.

But Brandi refused to take it.

"Hey, follow me," she said.

She left her books on the table, and he followed her to the corner of the room where he saw a couple of blankets and a pillow.

"Sit," she said. "I need a break. Keep me company."

Ravi wasn't sure what kind of drugs she was on, but he could make out that she wasn't sober, and it wasn't because she was tired. She kept looking around the room so that she didn't have to look directly at Ravi, and she lay down so he wouldn't notice the lack of control she had over her body.

"Sorry I missed you earlier today," Ravi said. "I was out walking."

Brandi closed her eyes.

"Kind of scary up here," Ravi said.

"I like it. This is kind of like my hiding spot. If you don't know where I am or you can't get in touch with me, don't come here—I'm hiding."

She kept her eyes closed and started telling Ravi stories about when she was younger, living with her sister and parents. They would be in the backyard on a sunny day, and Brandi would be on a swing attached to a branch of a tree that hung over from the neighbor's yard. Her mother would be pushing her, while her sister, Emily would be on a blanket on the grass, reading aloud the current book for school. Brandi never understood them, but she liked the sound of her sister's voice mixed in with the creaking of the swing's chain rubbing against the tree branch.

Brandi said that, in the summer, the family would take trips to the beach in California where they would rent a condo and stay there for a week. She remembered lying in the sand with her favorite red and white bathing suit, watching her family play in the Pacific.

"I love the ocean," Brandi said. "But I never wanted to be in it. I just wanted to listen to it, smell it, and fall asleep to it. And you know, if you put your ear to the Pacific, and listen really closely, you can hear a seashell."

Brandi's sense of nostalgia matched the somber tone of the library, her words filling in the tight gaps between the books on the shelves. She talked about when she was in high school and how she was friends with everyone, but she was sad because she never kept in touch with any of them.

"It's just strange," Brandi said. "I mean, we spend all these years together—some I knew even before high school, every day, for seven or eight hours, boyfriends, dances, parties, football games, movies, sleepovers—and then, all of a sudden, everything vanishes. Everything changes. You turn to your right, and all you see are memories, and that's all."

Ravi realized that the Brandi he had met the first time at the bar was not the same Brandi he was talking to at the library. She was quiet, pensive, and sad—she would have kept her pink coat instead of handing it to him. She loved the past more than the present. Her eyes remained closed as she turned her body away from Ravi, lying in the fetal position.

"Those days spent in the backyard and at the beach were the happiest my family had been. Nothing was wrong. We all smiled, and that was it. Now there is always something wrong."

Ravi didn't say anything.

"Sing me a song," Brandi whispered.

"What's that?"

"Sing me a song."

"I can't sing," Ravi said. "I have a horrible voice."

"Great," she said. "Those are the best. Now come on, sing."

Ravi sang what first came into his mind which was Tupac's "Dear Mama." He didn't know all the words, but he made them up as he sang. By the time he finished, Brandi was asleep. Ravi went back to her table to get her belongings, but before bringing them back, he looked in her purse. The caffeine pills she was talking about before were quite the opposite. They were painkillers—Lortab. She had two small capsules of them, labeled, not by a pharmacy, but by her handwriting. He had never taken any pills before, despite always being around them, but he took one then and swallowed it with Brandi's bottle of water which wasn't just a bottle of water, but more of a vodka tonic.

Realizing that she was not this happy, love-life kind of person all the time made Ravi feel better. It connected him to her, and he guessed it was the sadness he found in people that made him want to be with them. He went back to the corner and lay down next to Brandi, using the pink coat as his pillow. He was on his back, staring at the ceiling, seeing himself hanging from one of the sprinkler nozzles used to put out fires, waiting for the drug to close his eyes.

Brandi was still asleep when Ravi woke up early the next morning. He got about four hours of rest which was more than he had slept in months. He left her a note telling her that he had moved all of her belongings to the corner and that he'd hidden her purse under the blanket just by her head. Ravi also left a duplicate note on the table where she'd been studying the night before, just in case she woke up confused.

Ravi went back to the apartment and thought about Brandi's drugged-up face, and her pimple and sagging eyes. He remembered her stories about her family, and it made him think about his own. Mother. Father. Auntie.

"Come back, Vavi."

18

"Hi Auntie," Ravi said.

"Ravi dear, how are you?"

"I'm fine. Just working and spending time with my friends."

"You know you can call sometime. I miss you. You know you're always welcome to come over and stay for a bit or for as long as you like."

"I know. I'm sorry I haven't called in a while."

"So, you have some friends now? That's great, dear."

"Yeah, yeah," he stuttered. "I have quite a few. They keep me busy. We go all over the place. Racing on go-karts, going out to clubs, playing chess at the coffee shops. It's great. We go out to watch movies and hang out at the beach in the evenings sometimes."

"Wow—that's wonderful to hear," Auntie said.

"You've been okay?"

"I'm well," she said. "I tend to my garden and keep up with the book club."

"Nice. Yeah, my friend, Matt is in a book club. I think they're reading some book by Jack Kerouac. He loves it. I think I'm going to read it sometime. I don't know, I may even join the book club he's in."

"Wonderful. I'm in the middle of reading *One Flew Over the Cuckoo's Nest*. I read it a long time ago but have forgotten everything. I'm enjoying it. Next month it's my turn to pick the book, and I think I'm picking something Indian, you know? Something like Tagore or Narayan. Maybe introduce everyone to the Indian authors."

"That sounds great, Auntie."

"So, do you have a girlfriend? I figured it's been a long

time. You must be in love. Oh, love."

"Well, there's this girl, Danielle, I've been seeing. We met at the bookstore. She's awesome. She has black hair and black eyes. Tanned skin. And she's at UW studying Business. We're learning how to knit together, and she's an incessant talker with such a soothing voice. Sometimes we go downtown and count all the taxis that pass by. We never really count them, but we just sit outside and talk forever. You would love her."

"I would love to meet her," Auntie said.

"Yeah, that would be great. Maybe we can come over sometime and have dinner at your house. She loves Indian food. Especially chicken tikka masala. And your tikka is the best."

"Yes, yes, do come over with Danielle. And I will most certainly make some tikka masala for you all. Delightful. And how is your brother? Have you all been keeping in touch?"

"I just saw Vavi the other day. He's well. For a homeless guy, he looks sharper than a CEO. He asks about you every time I see him. Really, he's doing great. But one day, I hope to convince him to move in with me."

"Send him my love, my dear. And tell him that he always has a bed here. And you do, too."

"I know. Thanks, Auntie."

"Do you need anything? Food? Money?"

"I'm good. Thank you."

"There isn't a day where I don't think of you two. I really do wish we can spend more time together. I know you have a new life, with new friends and a job, but please, dear, maybe one Sunday, you and Danielle should come over."

"That would be great, Auntie. We'll do that soon."

He hated lying to Auntie.

19

Ravi thought he had quit his job. It wasn't so much that he had quit, but he just never went back. He hadn't gone to work in two weeks, and he didn't feel like calling Randy or putting in his two-week notice. The grocery store would call this a voluntary resignation. Ravi wasn't too worried about financial stability—he had gotten a lot of money from his parents after their death, and he hadn't used it yet. And at the same time, Ravi's aunt had been helping him out. When he moved into his apartment, his aunt left some money for him—nine thousand dollars in the bank. If he did happen to use up all his savings, he would be okay for at least a year using Auntie's gift.

He felt his body, his mind, searching, but he didn't know what he was searching for, like looking for the light switch in a dark room one he had never been in before. It must have been the stability he was looking for; it must have been contentment and closure of his parents' death and his brother's refusal to accept reality. It must have been the love Brandi had mentioned the first time they met.

Ravi hadn't called Brandi, nor had he seen her since the library. She hadn't called him, either. Ravi wanted to, but he was in such a slump, he didn't want to do anything. For the past week, he had pretty much just stayed at his apartment and dreamt about hanging himself in Ghost Town. His sleep hadn't gotten any better, and every time he brushed his teeth, he saw the dark shades underneath his eyes spreading. He thought he would have gotten fatter because he didn't exercise anymore, but his eating routine was thrown off—half a bowl of Ramen noodles for lunch and the other half for dinner. He hadn't shaved either, and his beard was full grown, itchy, and thick. Ravi had become a piece of paper with ink scribbled all over it.

After a week of hibernating, he shaved and finally left his apartment. He went walking around seven at night and visited a coffee shop not too far from his apartment. He thought about going to the grocery store to tell everyone that he was okay, but he couldn't get himself to go back. The café was one of his favorites. There was never a large crowd at night which made the place quiet, and he never had to take a book there to read because the café had shelves full of books for customers. He had either read or skimmed through all the books that he thought would be interesting, but he hadn't been there in a while—he was curious to see if they had any new books.

Ravi's favorite spot in the café was right next to the windows where the tables were just large enough for one person to sit. They were taller than the normal tables, and because of this, stools with cushioned backings were used rather than normal chairs. The large windows protruded out toward the sidewalk so that whoever was sitting there looked like they were on display. The lighting in the café was also the way Ravi liked it—bright. Most of the ones he'd gone to kept their lights dim to add atmosphere, but he didn't like this arrangement. Apart from his own apartment, he liked good and bright lighting.

He ordered a mocha and found a seat next to a window where he left his drink to cool and browsed through the shelves. He couldn't find anything new, so he walked to the back of the café where there were more shelves. These shelves were new—he hadn't seen them there before. As he made his way to the new books, he noticed a group of people sitting at one of the tables in the back, talking and laughing loudly.

Before he could look for any new books, he heard

someone call his name from the table. Ravi pretended that he didn't hear the voice, but she called his name again. He turned around and saw Brandi sitting at the table with the loud group of people. He waved and turned around back toward the shelves. He didn't know what to do. He wouldn't mind talking to Brandi, but not in front of her friends. He felt a tap on his shoulder and turned back around. Brandi stood before him with a brilliant smile. She wore gray sweatpants and a white T-shirt. He could see her blue bra underneath. Her hair was tied in a bun, and she didn't have any makeup on her face. He wanted to kiss her on the cheek.

"Hey," she said. "It has been too long. I was wondering about you."

"Yeah?" Ravi replied.

He shifted between looking at her and the books on the shelf.

"I came here to see if they have any books I might be interested in," he explained unnecessarily.

"I like this place," Brandi said. "I come here sometimes to read, just when I want to be by myself. But today I came here to meet up with some friends. You know, people you like and talk to and relate to?"

Ravi looked at the ceiling lights and then at their glare on the marble floor.

"I see you've taken a liking to your new pink coat," Brandi said.

Ravi just realized that he had been wearing the coat every day since the day Brandi had given it to him. He would put it on every morning without thinking, just like he was tying his shoelaces. He tried to say something to Brandi, but nothing came out.

"Hey," Brandi said, stepping closer to him.

He smelled the same body lotion that she wore the first time they met. The scent of strawberries permeated his body. He could barely look her in the eyes, and he tried not to picture her as he did that night Caroline and Eric were having sex.

"Why don't you come sit with us for a bit? We can catch up."

Ravi looked at the table and saw three guys sitting with two other girls.

"It's so good to see you," she said.

She hugged him and gently rubbed his chest with her hand.

"I think I'll just read for a bit."

"Come on," Brandi replied. "Just for a bit."

Her eyes were red. He didn't answer and looked at the floor and then at the bookshelf. Brandi understood his shyness and asked him if he would like to sit with her at another table, just the two of them. He agreed, and she took his hand and led him to another table. She introduced Ravi to her friends as they walked by. They didn't shake hands. All three guys wore plain black T-shirts and jeans. One guy had a thin mustache and long brown hair tied in a ponytail. The other two guys had short black hair and were clean-shaven. One of the girls wore a blue T-shirt, and the other girl wore a red one, both had the name of some band printed across each of them. The one with the blue shirt had spiky hair with the tips dyed in red, and the other girl wore thin-framed glasses and a lip ring. This was what Ravi noticed as he walked by. The guys barely nodded their heads at him and continued to talk to the girls. Ravi glanced at the girls again, but they didn't look at him.

Brandi and Ravi sat two tables away from her friends. They didn't talk at first. Conversations coming from the surrounding tables were heard in between the whirring sounds of the espresso machine. Ravi squinted and looked at the shelves. He wanted to look at them. He was just as nervous as that night at the bar, if not more—trying to keep his knees from shaking and silently taking deep breaths to slow down his heartbeat. Brandi twirled her hair, and her thoughts seemed to be off into the universe, and Ravi, like Brandi, fell into a daydream. He was hanging in Ghost Town until he felt a tap on his shoulder.

"Ravi," Brandi said. "You look spaced out."

"Really? Yeah, I guess I'm tired or something. Anyway, what's been going on?"

She told him that she had been busy with work and painting, and she didn't mention anything about the night at the UW library. She seemed dedicated to her art, as she talked about it with gestures and wide eyes, her lips never stopping. She played with her hair, and Ravi continued to shake his knees. He told her he had a copy of *All Quiet on the Western Front* for her if she was interested.

"I would love to read it," Brandi said. "But maybe when things slow down a bit. Oh, and you're always welcome to borrow any books from me, too."

"Nice coat Pink-O," one of Brandi's friends shouted from the other table.

They all laughed, and Ravi smiled and looked at Brandi. She told him that her friend was just joking.

A few seconds later, Ravi replied: "Yeah, I really like it."

But they didn't hear him.

"So, how's the grocery store going?" Brandi asked.

"Okay. Hey, I think I'm going to go now."

"What? Wait, we haven't even talked yet. Come on, just be patient. You need to practice talking to people, having conversations, and so on, and I'm the perfect person to practice with you."

It was amazing how well she knew him, he thought when they'd only been talking to each other for just a short bit. Ravi could tell that she was the nurturing sort.

"I thought about having sex with you not too long ago—I closed my eyes, and I thought about you."

Silence. She looked away, behind her, to the side of Ravi. She fiddled with her fingers, doing the itsy-bitsy spider, and bit her lip.

"Well," she said. "I've never heard a compliment like that before. That's sweet."

She didn't look at him when she spoke but at her hands. He waited for her to make eye contact, but she didn't look up, and then Ravi realized what he had just said.

"Oh, man. Look. I'm so sorry. I don't know why I said that. That's so horrible."

He felt the blood rush to his face, and he looked up to see if the ceiling fans were on, but the ceiling was bare. He sat back and distanced himself from her, but she leaned in more onto the table—she hadn't looked up at him yet. Ravi told her again that he was sorry, rubbing his thigh from the hip to the kneecap, trying not to look at her. She looked up at him.

"I really didn't mean to," Ravi said. "I should be going."

He pushed the chair back with his legs as he stood up. He thought she was mad at him, or that he'd made her feel awkward. He moved his hands back and forth because if he kept them still, she would see them shaking uncontrollably.

"Wait," Brandi said. "Don't go. Don't be embarrassed."

"Sorry."

"Don't be. It really is a sweet thing to say. Honestly."

She stood up and kissed him on the cheek. *Remarkable*, Ravi thought. She was remarkable. And he didn't know what this feeling was, but he assumed that he was falling in love. Just by that simple peck on the cheek, he was falling in love. That could be the only explanation for the odd sensation buzzing around in his head, his stomach, legs, and arms. It consumed Ravi from within. For a few seconds, he noticed nothing else around him. He wasn't in the café. Brandi's friends were not sitting at the table behind them. The bookshelves, the whirring espresso machine—none of those things were there. It was just him and her in a world of void. Brandi brought Ravi back to reality with a tap on the shoulder.

"You want to go for a walk?"

"Sure," Ravi said.

They walked back toward the front of the café. She didn't say bye or where she was going to her friends at the other table. Ravi grabbed the mocha he had left at the front of the café and took a sip—it was too cold to drink, and he threw it away as they walked outside, her hand holding his. They didn't talk for a few minutes. Instead, they looked through the windows of the stores they walked by.

"Thanks for visiting me at the library. I was having a bad night."

"No problem. You feeling better?"

"You know, I was hoping that you would give me a call," Brandi said. "I feel bad for trying to get in touch with you all the time."

"I'm sorry. I really did mean to call you."

"So, what happened?" she asked.

"I don't know. I just didn't want to talk to anyone. I quit my job and just stayed home for a couple of weeks."

"What's wrong with you?" she asked.

"I'm fine. Just in a phase, I guess."

He pictured kissing her and taking her shirt off. She looked just as pretty, not all dressed up like when they first met at the bar. They reached the end of the block, and the pedestrian light gave them the sign to walk across. A bicyclist jolted around the corner and crashed into both Brandi and Ravi. The bike turned over, and the guy fell to the ground. One of the wheels caught Ravi on the back of his calf. The burning sensation lasted for a few seconds. The cyclist stood up and brushed the dirt off his clothes. Ravi looked at Brandi who was okay, and then he looked at the bicyclist who was mumbling something. He got back on his bike and rode off. Brandi laughed.

"Wow. If I was with my ex right now, that guy would already have been beaten to pieces."

"Can't care less, I guess," Ravi said. "Just accidents."

"Just a laid-back kind of guy. I like that."

"Yeah, I guess that's a way to look at it. Mainly, I just don't care. He could have torn my leg off and I wouldn't have cared. I just don't care anymore."

"I don't know why," Brandi said. "You should care. It makes you feel important. It gives you something to think about."

She skipped and hopped.

"And it makes others feel important, too. It's almost selfish, you know? Not caring. Take the world, man."

She made things so simple.

"I talked to my ex the other day," Brandi said. "We've been broken up for about a year, but we still keep in touch with each other on and off."

Brandi told Ravi that they were together for three years in a close relationship, and she caught him cheating on her and ended the relationship.

"I can't tell you how tough it was," she said. "I loved him. I really did, but he had cheated on me too many times, and too many times is enough."

Her eyes watered, and she pushed her body close to Ravi's as they continued to walk.

"Tell me about your girlfriends," Brandi said.

"I've never had one. You should know that, seeing that you know me so well in just a brief time. And yes, I'm still a virgin."

"Really?" Brandi replied. "Not even one? Is it because you're Indian? Shivali couldn't date either."

She was right in some sense. A lot of Indian families didn't agree with dating, especially the older generations, especially Americans. But that was not the case with Ravi. His parents wouldn't have minded. Mother always told him to be open to the people he would meet. "You can fall in love without knowing it," she would say. He just never dated. Ravi explained this to Brandi.

"I see," she said. "So, are you just shy? I just don't understand why you never had a girlfriend."

"I've been on a couple of dates."

"A couple—wow, that's really going for it. On my first date, I went on a couple of dates. You're crazy. You're not normal."

Ravi thought for a few seconds as they continued to walk. She held his hand. He thought about pressure—should I squeeze harder? Should I let go? How long do we hold hands? Wait, why was she holding my hand? He didn't want to let go.

He told her about his last date, in high school, with Jessica. She asked him out one night and they went to an expensive restaurant, her favorite restaurant. It was a French place, and with Ravi's allowance, all he could afford was a Coke and a salad. He was nervous, noticing every movement he made, every cough, every squeak in his voice. Everybody around them magnified, the world became large, and he could see the calcium deposits on their teeth. Jessica was polite. She wore a dark purple dress—long black hair, black eyes, and large lips that stretched from one side of her face to the other. Easily kissable. They were right there, right in front of his face, staring at him. It was well-known in high school that she was a sensual being. She would constantly lick her lips and lean into where he could see her cleavage. And as soon as he had calmed down and settled into the night, he just could not listen to her talk about gymnastics and getting drunk and Billy and Brian and exquisite gourmet and whatever else she was talking about. His mind drifted, and in walked a cute blue dinosaur.

Ravi felt bad after the date had finished, as he was sure he wasn't the most interesting person—he had simply responded yes and no to everything she said. He didn't know why he was there. Why they were there? Why she'd asked him out. And before Ravi knew it, they were at her door. He shook her hand while she was trying to hug him. He felt like a jerk. That was his last date. Then he told Brandi about his interest in Annie.

"Well, I know that all dates can't be perfect," she said. "And I understand that you could be nervous, but you need to do more of these things. You can't just go around dreaming about dinosaurs when the love of your life could be right in front of you."

"Yeah, I know," Ravi said. "It just happens. Guess I'm just not used to these kinds of things."

"Well, what, are you thinking about dinosaurs now?" she asked.

"Not at all."

"Good. Whatever happened to Annie?"

Brandi stared at the ground as they walked. He told her how Annie had left without telling anyone.

"Did you like her?" Brandi asked. "You know what I mean."

Her curiosity made Ravi happy. She asked him in that tone like she wanted to know where he stood with Annie—if he was in love with her. She was probing to see where she and Ravi could go in their relationship. Though he'd never been with anyone, he had been around enough girls and guys to know what these questions meant. He told Brandi that he liked being around Annie, enjoyed her friendship and that if anything would have happened, he would have been happy with it. He said that Annie was the only person who gave him attention, some show of affection, and how he fell in love with her lip gloss at the grocery store when they were playing hide and seek.

"But what about me?" Brandi asked. "I give you attention."

She scrunched her shoulders and spoke in a high tone as if she had just jumped into a cold swimming pool.

"Oh, definitely," Ravi said. "I mean this was all up until I had met you, you strange abnormal person."

"You're the strange one, walking around dreaming about dinosaurs," Brandi said. "Well, I'm sorry about Annie. Not to sound dumb, but sometimes that's just the way it is."

"Tupac," Ravi said.

"Exactly," she replied. "Did you think about her the same way you thought about me the other day?"

"No. I guess I never did."

Ravi could tell that she liked what she heard by the way she smiled. As they continued walking, they took a break from talking, and he thought about the time he and Vavi were at the museum when Ravi was a child.

"Okay, Ravi, you remember this one? Do you remember this one from your dinosaur encyclopedia? Look at its teeth and its arms. Right. Right."

"Twyaneraurus Rex."

"Yes. Good. Very good. You have a sharp memory, Ravi. These are all dinosaur bones—they're called fossils, and they're the actual bones that were inside dinosaurs a long time ago."

"Do you remember how long they can get? Think hard. You read about it not too long ago."

"Forty feet."

"Wow. Particularly good. And what about this one? Look at the picture. Do you see its three bones and its hard shell? Now, what do you think that is?"

"Twyceratops."

"Oh, and this one you know. I don't even have to ask."

"Maiasaura."

"What does that mean, Ravi?"

"Good Mother. Good Lizard."

"Yes. Wow, Ravi, you know your dinosaurs. Excellent job. Good memory. Let's go find Mother and Father so you can tell them what you just told me."

Brandi brought Ravi back to the present.

"You're missing out. You realize that, right?" Brandi said. "I mean, what about other stuff and all that? You know, has anyone ever gone down on you? Have you ever gone down on someone? Have you ever made it past the bra? Past the underwear? Tell me something, Ravi—tell me something."

Her voice was filled with curiosity and amusement. Ravi almost felt like a science experiment, but he could see why she was so bewildered. He thought about Annie at the grocery store, hiding in the flower department. He didn't know why, but he answered her. Things he had kept to himself his whole life, things he hadn't told his brother about, he told Brandi. She was so upfront and sweet about it, Ravi didn't mind. And just talking about these things with her had gotten him excited.

"Just once."

Brandi's eyes widened as she placed her hands on top of her head. She hopped up and down as they walked, shouting "wow," repeatedly. After she calmed down, he saw her noticing the zipper of his pants, and he placed his hands in his pockets. Brandi smiled and gave him a nudge.

"Oh Ravi," she said. "What am I going to do with you? I don't think I've met anyone like you. Ravi. Ravi. Ravi."

"Well, there's something I haven't told you yet," he said.

"What is it? I want to know so badly—there must be so much more. This is fun."

Ravi paused and took a long breath and then another one.

"What, Ravi? What is it?"

He told her about how his parents were killed.

Vavi and Ravi were going to meet them at the Egyptian, the movie theater downtown, to watch *Amélie*. It was around six in the evening—they were home, throwing a football outside in the backyard while their parents were already downtown shopping. They didn't hear the phone ring when their mother had called, but when they both went inside to get a drink, they saw the small red light on the answering machine blinking. Vavi pressed the play button while he sipped orange-flavored Gatorade. Mother was asking the brothers to go meet them at the movie theater in about an hour and a half. This gave them some time to shower, eat a small dinner, and then take the bus to the Egyptian. They arrived early, and they were surprised by the extensive line forming in front of the theater. It formed a barrier, dividing the sidewalk in half, and nothing could be seen on the other side of the line. From the bus stop, Ravi and Vavi started running toward the theater to get in line just in case their parents hadn't gotten in line yet. The queue had curved so that it wouldn't protrude onto the street, and after about five minutes of standing, the line started to move. The brothers slowly arrived at the point where they could see the other side of the sidewalk. About a block down, Ravi saw an ambulance with red lights in motion parked on the side of the road. There were also several police officers. Ravi didn't think anything of it—he just thought it was a bad car accident. He looked at Vavi who was anxiously looking around for their parents.

Ravi could smell buttered popcorn coming from inside the movie hall, wavering through the air. The employees must have just popped a fresh batch, getting ready for the rush for the next showing. Ravi couldn't wait for that bag of popcorn and a Coke. Their parents always bought them a snack to eat while they watched a movie. Vavi didn't like eating the popcorn all too much, but he always got a box of Junior Mints. It had been a while since they all had watched a movie, so the experience felt close to going to the theater for the first time.

As they moved closer to the box office, Vavi grabbed Ravi's hand, and they took off running. He was running so fast, that Ravi couldn't keep up and fell onto the sidewalk, tearing his khaki pants right around the kneecaps. Vavi came back and helped him stand back up. He told Ravi to hurry, in a faint voice, almost a whisper. Ravi didn't ask any questions and ran as fast as he could. Vavi was ahead of him, and he had stopped at the ambulance site.

Ravi got there, but he couldn't see anything. There was a crowd of people huddled around a yellow caution tape. Ravi pushed his way through until he recognized Vavi's back and gave him a slight nudge. When he turned around, Ravi saw his large, round, watery eyes. He pushed his brother aside.

Their heads were leaning against the wall of some kitchen store. Father was in his slacks, and he wore his favorite gray jacket. His polished black shoes were pointing toward the sky. On his left arm, Ravi could see the silver watch Vavi had given him for his birthday. Mother was on the other side of him. Ravi couldn't see much of her body, but he recognized the necklace she had around her neck, and her shoes had been knocked off. The navy blue high heels were on the curb of the sidewalk near the ambulance. This was all Ravi could recognize of his parents. Their heads were completely smashed in, propped against the wall. Blood stained the sidewalk, their clothes, and the wall. Father's skull was completely open, and his insides were coming out. Vavi held Ravi close to his body. Vavi, as hard as he was trying to hold it back, started to cry, and as soon as Ravi saw his brother cry, he started to cry, as well.

Ravi ended the story there. He didn't cry when he told Brandi—he had become too numb to let those feelings choke him around the neck. He had been looking at the ground as he was describing the event to Brandi, and when he looked up, he saw that they were standing outside Brandi's house.

Brandi was completely silent. She was sniffling a bit, but she was holding in her tears. Ravi could barely look at her in the face and stared at the ground again. He felt bad because he didn't tell her the story to make her sad or to gain some sympathy or attention. He just wanted to let her know why he turned out the way he was now.

He looked at the house and saw that the balls of yarn were still in the basket outside her red door. They hadn't talked for the last couple of minutes. She stopped sniffling when they got to the door. She managed to ask him about Vavi, and he told her that he was okay, but that he was homeless, living not too far from where the murder took place. She asked Ravi more about what had happened, and Ravi said that it took the police a few weeks to find the killers and that they had used baseball bats. Neither Vavi nor Ravi went to the trial, but Auntie went, and she would fill them in about the killers—they were two skinny men in their late twenties, both with brown hair and goatees. They were brothers. They said they didn't intend to kill Mother and Father. They were on acid at the time, as well, and later that day, they had beaten another couple for money, but they weren't killed.

Brandi hugged Ravi and put her hands against his face like she was going to kiss him. Ravi didn't move. She hugged him like she needed to be hugged more than Ravi did, and he gave her a strong embrace, and her wet nose swiped his shoulder. He didn't wipe it off.

"I'm sorry," Brandi said. "I don't know what to say."

"There's nothing much to say. It happened years ago. It's okay now."

"But is it?"

Brandi told him that, if he ever needed to talk to her about it, she would be willing to listen. He wanted to kiss her on the tip of her nose. She kept her face close to his, and they didn't talk for a few seconds, and then she apologized for crying all over him. She asked him to come inside. Ravi didn't want to go inside, but the way she looked at him with her glossy eyes and the way she hugged him and touched his chin with her fingertips compelled him. She had put him in a trance.

Brandi kept her place neat and clean. The living room had a light blue sofa with a matching recliner and a square, wooden coffee table was in the middle of the room. A dining table separated the living room from the kitchen. Her place was bright. On the walls were prints of famous art pieces by Picasso, Van Gogh, and Monet, and there was a shelf full of books near the hallway. The entertainment center was against the wall opposite the sofa. Everything was in its place. He had imagined it to be completely different—dark, somber lighting, with canvases, paint tubes, and brushes strewn about the room, but it was quite the opposite. He told her that he loved her place as he sat on the sofa trying to cheer her up. She sat next to him on the sofa and turned on the television.

"I rarely get to watch any TV," Brandi said. "I don't even know what's on these days."

"Yeah, I don't watch too much either."

She repeatedly changed the channel. Ravi was thinking about her, and he liked to think that she was thinking about him, as well. He realized that he was breathing loudly through his nose, so he opened his mouth. Then he realized that she was breathing loudly through her nose. Brandi shifted toward him and put her head on his lap, and without hesitation, Ravi caressed her hair. He had never done that before, but it felt natural—that his hand should be combing through her hair, and that his other hand should be on her shoulder.

They didn't kiss. He just continued to caress her hair and stare blankly at the television set. A few minutes later, Brandi fell asleep on his lap. She woke up to take off her shirt, and she went back to sleep on Ravi's lap. Ravi looked at her blue bra—it matched Picasso's *The Old Guitarist* hanging on the wall. It matched her eyes. It matched her sadness. Her tanned chest was sprinkled with freckles. He wanted to connect the dots and kiss each one. He wondered what she was dreaming about. Was she envisioning his parents, bloodied and battered, on the sidewalk? Was she thinking about her ex-boyfriend? Was she dreaming about him? Ravi kissed her on the cheek and gently lifted her head and put the sofa pillow underneath her head so he could slip out. Near the sofa, there was a basket full of woven blankets. He took one out and placed it over her and went back to his apartment.

20

Back at the apartment, Ravi lay in bed with his eyes open, staring at the ceiling. Brandi had become a spectacle to him, and he didn't know how—they'd only seen each other a few times, yet she had somehow managed to become ingrained in his thoughts. He had given her more information than he had to anyone else he knew. There was something about that, something about the releasing of secrets and pain to someone else, that was comforting. He'd let her in without really knowing it.

Realizing that he wouldn't be able to go to sleep any time soon, Ravi thought about his mother. Every morning, after mother showered, she would go into her bedroom with her body wrapped in one towel and her hair in another, and she would stand in front of the dresser. On top of the dresser were small pictures and statues of Indian gods—Krishna, Ganesh, Vishnu, and Brahma. Woven throughout these gods were marigold petals. She would light incense, place her clasped-together hands in front of her face, and bow her head. Ravi would peer around the door and watch her pray as the incense made its way throughout the room to his eyes, causing them to water. She would never see him, and he never told her that he watched her pray. Her morning ritual would last no more than five minutes. Ravi thought that she was the only one who was religious in their family. Father was an atheist, but a quiet one. Their parents were somewhat strict, and they never forced any kind of religion onto their kids, but they wanted to instill a good work ethic and teach them how to be kind and how to be respectful to others. Ravi rarely thought about God, religion, and so on. He guessed that watching his mother pray was his closest relationship with a god.

Vavi never outwardly expressed any religious views, but he had a couple of versions of the Gita on his bookshelf and a few books on Hinduism and Christianity, too. There was still something spiritual about him, but Ravi didn't think Vavi really meant to be like that. It was just natural.

He remembered the time when he and his parents had gone to a high school basketball game to watch Vavi play. He was a talented player. He didn't score much, but he took the opportunity when it arose, and Ravi rarely saw him make a turnover. The team was rather good. They never won any championships or tournaments or anything, but they always gave the fans something to cheer about.

At the end of one game, Ravi remembered hearing the squeaking of basketball shoes rubbing against the court, hearing the opposing team's fans shouting "defense" while the other fans shouted "offense," and the huge ceiling lights made a strong glare on the floor. Little brothers and sisters ran along the sideline and cheered their siblings on while the coaches ran along the same sideline scolding their players. In that game, amidst its chaos, every time Vavi's team had the ball, he would stand in the corner. He wouldn't move on offense. Vavi just stood in the corner, like he had found his quiet spot like he was praying on a battlefield in the middle of a war.

The score was tied, and there were only about twenty seconds left in the game. Excitement and tension could be felt traveling from the players on the court to the players sitting on the bench to the coach to the parents in the stands. While Vavi's team had the ball, they moved all around the court. "Pass and cut, pass and cut," the coach told them, and the team was passing and cutting and waiting until the last seconds of the game to take the shot— except for Vavi.

Finally, one of the players drove to the basket, attracting the defense's attention, and he passed the ball to Vavi. Everyone had forgotten about him, standing in the corner as if he was shunning society. Vavi caught the ball and shot it without hesitation. His team won the game with that shot, and the team, the coach, and the fans were all shouting with joy. But Vavi remained standing in the corner of the court for a few more seconds like he wasn't ready to leave that spot—like he hadn't quite finished praying yet. He was surrounded by his teammates slapping him on the back of the head and pushing him around, congratulating him for the shot he'd taken. Vavi barely broke a smile and stared down at the floor. And it wasn't until after the whole team was back in the locker room that he moved from his spot and walked back to the locker room, himself—walking as if he had just had an epiphany, and everything before him, surrounding him, made sense. He was in his own world.

The ride back home was quiet. Everyone spoke sparingly, talking only about what to eat for dinner. It was like Mother and Father knew that Vavi was going to make that shot, or that they knew that Vavi was going through a spiritual experience on the court. Ravi was the only one who wanted to push him around and give him a big hug just as his teammates had done.

Ravi had seen several other random moments like that one when Vavi appeared to be in his own world, deep in thought, acknowledging his existence in the world, such as when he was playing at the arcade or kicking the soccer ball around, or when they were eating at a restaurant or exercising in the weight room. Ravi hadn't seen it since the death of their parents, though—that look in his eyes and that motion in his body where everything was in control. But Vavi was purposely homeless—there was something spiritual about this, with the concept of blending in with the environment, becoming one with his surroundings. Even though he was drunk most of the time, he still seemed to have control over his body, his thoughts, and his world.

Ravi was hanging again. Flashes of Brandi in her blue bra and sweatpants flickered in between, but in the end, he saw himself in Ghost Town with the rope around his neck and the cowboy hat on the wooden boards below his dangling feet. He wished someone was around to watch him hang.

He still couldn't sleep, so he went to the closet and shuffled through some boxes until he found the one he was looking for in the corner of the closet, tucked under old shirts and pants he didn't wear anymore. He opened the box and took out the only thing that it held—an old answering machine wrapped in one of Mother's saris. The cloth was gold and green, embroidered with roses around the edges. He smelled the sari—it still had the faint smell of her perfume and the smell of the Indian store where she had bought it, or maybe he just wanted to remember those scents so badly that they came to him in memory only, and he just didn't realize that it was all gone. He stared at the answering machine, rubbed his fingers across its top, and then plugged it into the outlet on the wall. After a few seconds, the red light came on, and the tape made the rewinding sound. Giving a deep sigh, Ravi pressed play.

Ravi-Vavi, where are you two? Anyway, just calling to let you know that Father and I are going to the 7:30 showing of Amélie at The Egyptian—that one hall theater downtown. I hear it's a funny show. Come join us, please.

Her voice had a hint of a British accent. She had always held herself like a lady with Audrey Hepburn charm. Whenever his parents had parties at the house, everyone would surround her in awe and listen to her talk, mesmerized by her lady-like voice. She talked with precision and with direction—everything she said led to something important or funny. Father would smile and look at her as she talked to the crowd, his love for her revealed in his teeth.

And boys, please shower if you do come because I know you all are outside playing sports. If we don't see you there, we'll see you tonight at the house. Father says hi. Okay, love you, bye.

He played the message over and over. Rewind. Play. *Love you.* Rewind. Play. *Love you.* Rewind. Play. *Love you.* He kissed the machine. *Ravi-Vavi, Ravi-Vavi, Ravi-Vavi.*

21

Ravi and Brandi were eating dinner at Tacos Express. She had left a message on his answering machine earlier that day to go meet her there at 7:00.

"I got something for you," she said.

She grabbed her school bag and pulled out a cell phone and handed it to him.

"A cell phone?"

"Yeah, it's my dad's, but he doesn't use it anymore. He uses the one work gives him. Thought you'd maybe like it. Maybe it will help you to give me a call one day."

"Thanks, but I don't think I'll use it."

"Why?"

"I don't know, just not yet."

Brandi looked at the phone and then looked away toward the people ordering their food at the counter. Ravi took a small bite out of his taco, which was all he could manage for the rest of the night.

Silence.

"Do you not want to keep in touch with me? Is that it?"

"No, not at all. Not at all. I'll use it, just give me some time."

"You know," Brandi said, "I wasn't always like this."

"Like what?"

"Like an artist, being skeptical about everything, always wanting to be miserable."

"You're miserable?"

"You saw those pictures at my house—I used to be a cheerleader in high school. I was a part of all those clubs, and I was even prom queen. Kind of strange, don't you think? Look at me now—all drab, surrounded by friends who hate the world. I used to laugh and smile a lot, you know."

"I don't think it's strange," Ravi said.

"That's why I have a cell phone. I don't want to be one of those people who refuses to accept technology, like my friends. You know, kill-your-television type of people."

"But why the change? What made you do that?"

"I guess it was after high school. Everyone left, and with the constant pressure from my parents—I just started changing. I met new friends, started getting interested in what they were into, and started acting like them. I hated myself for doing that—for letting others influence me, making me act a way I don't want to be."

Ravi thought that she was mainly referring to her ex-boyfriend.

"But I'm getting back to myself, I think. And you know, despite how much I get on you for not opening up, I understand why you don't. I'm not saying it's good, but I understand."

"Well," Ravi said. "I would rather keep to myself than force myself into being someone I don't want to be."

Brandi frowned—her eyebrows were almost vertical. She had taken offense, though Ravi didn't mean to hurt her feelings.

"We all have our ways of finding ourselves," she said, not looking at Ravi, but at her hands, fiddling with a drinking straw.

She changed moods and told him about how she was enjoying the book she was reading which was Faulkner's *Light in August*. He listened to her talk and watched her eyes light up and her arms move around as she described it. Ravi had read the book, but he didn't tell her. He would rather hear her talk because she was so excited about it. He realized that, though he had never called her before, he was tracing her phone number with his index finger on the table. She changed subjects.

"My ex and I got in a pretty bad argument again the other day."

"Why are you getting into arguments with your ex?" Ravi asked. "That's why they are exes—you don't have to get in arguments with them anymore."

"You make it sound so simple."

Ravi looked at the cell phone on the table. He wanted it. He'd wanted it as soon as Brandi offered it to him. But he wasn't used to the idea of having a friend—one to hang out with and keep in touch with regularly.

She continued talking about her ex-boyfriend: "He wanted me to go on a road trip with him this summer, but I told him no because I wanted to concentrate on other things, instead, which is not even the real reason. The real reason is that I just don't want to go with him."

"Why do you still hang out with him?"

"Well, it may sound dumb, but we really did go through a lot together."

She described their time spent together over the past years—how he would hold her hand when they would sing karaoke together at the bar, or how at night they would find a scenic place like a hill looking over Seattle to park the car and listen to music while they talked about the future. They used to go running alongside the Puget Sound, go hiking, and they would go over to each other's family's houses for dinner. She wasn't his first, but he was her first.

"We were really close," Brandi said. "He had dreams of being a lawyer, and we even talked about being married and all, but then all of a sudden, he changed. He started getting increasingly mean, and he cheated on me. I don't know, I guess he was bored of me. It sucks to know when someone doesn't want to be around you anymore."

"Listen," Ravi said, "I don't think anyone could ever be bored of you. He's just a jerk who doesn't know any better. Forget him. Move on."

Move on. He knew he was being a hypocrite.

"You're too sweet," Brandi said and took a bite out of her chicken taco.

The guy ordering at the counter wore brown slacks with a glossy black belt, and a white button-up shirt, tucked in. He was thin but not sickly-looking, and his hair was neatly combed. Underneath his arm was a newspaper. This was the last thing Ravi saw before he felt the rope around his neck.

22

Ravi stopped by his former place of employment. It was his first time there since he had quit.

"Where have you been, son?" Randy asked.

Randy looked worn: his shirt was not tucked in; his black pants were wrinkled and the bottom parts dragged against the floor as he walked because he wasn't wearing his belt. His face was shaven but shaven like he had used a month-old razor. Ravi looked at his eyes, red and glossy, and his hair looked like the mop he held in his hands had been plopped on his head.

"Sorry," Ravi said. "Just had a lot of things going on."

"You could have called," Randy said.

"I know."

"We thought you pulled an Annie."

"I'm still here," Ravi said, looking at the ceiling.

"Do you still want to work?" Randy asked. "We could really use you."

"Not really. I can put in my two weeks' notice, though."

"Don't worry about it. Bill needs more hours anyway. He took most of yours these past few weeks."

"Tell him I said thanks," Ravi said.

Ravi told Randy bye and walked through the aisles looking for some snacks and drinks for the apartment. He checked out at the counter and walked back to the apartment, eyeing the flower department before leaving.

One night, Annie had helped Randy out and worked in the grocery section of the store instead of the flower department. One of the employees, Adrienne, never showed up for her shift, and Randy needed someone to fill her spot, but no one was available except for Annie. Ravi was already in the middle of his shift when she showed up. She didn't wear her uniform, but she wore a knee-length skirt and a dark blue T-shirt with something in Japanese written on it. As always, she didn't have any cosmetics on, and she wore large, plastic, black-framed glasses. Anyone could hear her walking from miles away because of the way she walked with her sandals slapping loudly against her heels. She wore a blue anklet laced with small bells, and they would jingle when she walked. Randy didn't even bother asking her to go back and change into her uniform because he knew that, if he did, she wouldn't come back. It was also her birthday. The store was empty that night, and it was just Annie, Bill, Ryan, and Ravi. Randy was in the office filling up paperwork. They played hide and seek for a good hour or so, though there weren't too many good hiding spots in the store. Ravi tried hiding in the beer coolers, but that didn't last too long, so before Ryan could catch him, he ran to the flower department and hid in the corner behind a large stack of flowerpots. He heard someone whispering, and he looked to the other corner and saw Annie hiding behind a batch of long-stemmed sunflowers. She darted over to Ravi's corner and pushed in close to him so that the pots could hide them both. Ravi didn't know Annie too well then. But this was the start of whatever kind of relationship they had. She breathed quietly to herself, but through her mouth, Ravi could smell the strawberry-flavored lip gloss that he always saw her rubbing on her mouth.

"Bill is in the bakery section underneath the table of cupcakes," she whispered. "Ryan will find him before he finds us. Get ready, because we may have to make another move."

She placed her arm on top of Ravi's to keep her balance as they continued to stay crouching down. Ravi kept looking at her anklet and her orange-painted toenails.

"You're very colorful," he whispered.

"Mom thinks I overdo it."

She looked around to see if Ryan was anywhere near, and then Ravi heard her whisper "damn." A customer was waiting to check out some items—she didn't have too many, and they wondered if they should try and help her or just wait to see if she would just leave after losing her patience. After about twenty seconds, Ravi ended up going to the checkout counter to help the lady. He was quick, scanning the toothpaste, the toilet paper, and the two bags of Sour Cream and Onion chips like they were all one product. He glanced over to the bakery section and saw Bill eating a donut. The lady paid with cash, and Ravi didn't check to see if he gave her the correct change. Before she could say thank you, Ravi took off back to the flower department where Annie was still hiding. She was trying so hard not to burst out laughing, because she couldn't believe that he was able to help the lady without being caught by Ryan. A few seconds later, Bill walked by holding a chocolate donut, and Ryan was walking behind him. He had been caught. Ryan, so far, hadn't thought to check the flower department, and Annie and Ravi remained hidden there for fifteen minutes.

To pass the time, they whispered to each other Six Degrees of Kevin Bacon. Annie was better than Ravi at the game, and though Ravi didn't know too many Kevin Bacon movies, he liked the game because it made Annie talk—he could smell the lip gloss coming from her breath. Finally, Ryan shouted in the middle of the store, "Okay, okay! I give up! Come out!" Annie and Ravi didn't leave immediately. They remained crouched down as Annie smelled the sunflowers, tulips, and roses surrounding her. She reminded Ravi of Ophelia in the painting of her floating dead in a body of water, but Annie looked like she was sleeping more than looking dead. He also thought she looked like the Maid Marian drew in the Robin Hood book he had read as a child. Just natural. Annie closed her eyes as she held her nose to each bud and breathed in deeply. "Come on, don't be shy," she said and motioned to him to smell the reds, blues, yellows, and oranges around them. He closed his eyes as she did and breathed in the scents, and on the last flower, a red rose, Ravi opened his eyes—Annie's face was directly in front of his. Lip to lip, nose to nose, and eye to eye. They were so close to each other that he couldn't see the color of her eyes or the pores on her face. They kissed with hesitance. Her hands were on his cheeks, and Ravi's were still holding the rose. It lasted for a few minutes, swaying their heads from side to side, moving their hands across each other's backs. She became the leader as she pushed his shoulders down, guiding him to lie on his back as she straddled on top of him. This was done in one motion, without taking a breath. He opened his eyes to see how she looked—her eyes were closed tightly, revealing small creases flowing on each side of her head, and her nose was pushed to the left as Ravi's was pushed to the right. *Something was odd about this—the way noses looked when kissing*, Ravi thought as he pushed his tongue against her gums. It reminded him of those cylindrical foam bars that kids used to play with in the swimming pool—the way they flop from side to side.

She moaned as Ravi's tongue glided on top of her tongue, barely touching the roof of her mouth. With the rose still in hand, and as he pushed her shirt up just above her belly button, Randy started shouting their names because Ryan was getting worried since they hadn't revealed themselves yet. Annie's head shifted backward, and Ravi's rested on the floor. She didn't say anything, and she stood up and walked away. Ravi remained on the floor, staring at the fluorescent ceiling lights, twirling the rose in his hand. He didn't get up for another five minutes, and when he walked to the center of the store where everyone else was standing, Annie was nowhere to be seen. They never talked about that kiss. She never brought it up, nor did Ravi, but he did leave the rose on the windshield of her car the next day.

As he walked up to his apartment thinking about that kiss at the grocery store, he saw Vavi holding his two garbage bags, standing outside the entrance to the building. He was looking up as if he was looking for Ravi through one of the windows. Ravi called his name. He turned around, wiped his hand on his pants, and shook Ravi's hand. Ravi had forgotten how tall his brother was—he hadn't seen him standing up in a long time.

"What's going on?" Ravi asked.

It took him some time to answer. He struggled to keep upright as he coughed deep from the lungs.

"Just thought I'd drop by and see where you live," Vavi said. "Looks nice from the outside."

"It's a good place. Do you want to come in? I'll show you around."

"Thanks, but I don't want to stampede," Vavi replied, smiling.

"Really, it's no problem."

"Thanks, but I'd rather not."

"Well. Let me bring these things upstairs, and then let's go get some coffee. I know a place that's open twenty-four hours."

"Yeah," Vavi said. "Let's do that."

Ravi quickly took the groceries inside and rushed back out. He wasn't sure if his brother would still be waiting for him, but Vavi was still there, standing on the curb, smoking a cigarette. They walked to Ravi's favorite coffee shop, the one where he had run into Brandi, and Vavi told him that he used to frequent the same place, but it had been a while since he'd been there.

"Do they still have the books there?" he asked.

"Yeah. Are you still into reading?"

Even though Vavi studied Psychology in school, his truest passion was English. He read all the time, wrote all the time, and always came up with ideas for possible novels. When they were at the house, his room was full of books and stacks of papers. That was all he had in his room. Ravi thought that he and Brandi would have a lot to talk about if they ever met.

"Yeah," Vavi said. "When I find one, I'll pick it up and read it. Haven't found anything good lately. What about you? You read anything good lately?"

"I used to read a lot at night when I couldn't sleep. But I haven't read anything lately."

"Man, you should see if you can find Philip K. Dick. He's unbelievable. I used to have one, but I think I gave it away or sold it a long time ago."

He quickly looked through his bags and then shook his head.

"I haven't heard of him, but I'll check him out next time."

They walked into the café and ordered their drinks. Vavi browsed through the shelves as Ravi waited for the mochas to be made.

"Here," Vavi shouted. "Here it is, Ravi. Philip. Philip."

He held the book up high so Ravi could see it across the room. Realizing that he had shouted across the room, causing people to raise their heads and look at him, he quickly put the book on the shelf, causing the shelf to rock, and the books from the top shelf to fall onto the floor. Vavi picked up three books and put them back on the shelf. As he bent down again to pick up some of the remaining books, he looked around and noticed that everyone was staring at him. He left the books on the floor and quickly walked to the outside sitting area, mumbling to himself, "Dick, Dick, Dick, Dick. Philip, Philip, Philip."

The temperature outside was in the mid-sixties. There was a slight breeze coming from Puget Sound. Ravi saw the pedestrians walk by, the cars drive by, and he knew that the world continued to rotate upon its imaginary axis, but as he sat with his brother and looked at his eyes, his skin, his mouth, his arms and legs, everything outside of where they sat ceased to exist. It was just them two having a couple of mochas and conversing. Ravi couldn't help but smile.

"What?" Vavi asked. "What are you smiling about?"

"Nothing."

There was a moment of silence. They both stared at the ground.

"You know," Ravi said. "There was a time when I really didn't think I would see you again. That you were gone forever."

"I'm sorry," Vavi replied. "But at some point, I would have come for you, to make sure you're okay. It's just that, when I needed my time alone, I became addicted to it. I found myself in a chasm or something you know. But really, there is never a day I don't think about you."

"I know."

"And we did end up finding each other. It was going to happen, you know."

"How's the homeless life going?" Ravi asked.

"It's interesting, you know," he said. "All my troubles revolve around making it through the day. The future I must worry about is tonight, and then tomorrow, I worry about that day's future. I get lonely, but I get enough talk from the people who walk by. As you can see, I drink too much."

"Do you plan to do this forever?" Ravi asked.

"I don't know. I haven't really thought about it. Been keeping busy with the script for now."

They sat, smoked cigarettes, and didn't talk for a while. It felt natural to Ravi. Only with his brother could he sit and not talk for hours and hours and still feel okay. Through this silence, they were somehow still communicating with each other. Ravi knew Vavi was thinking about his science-fiction screenplay, and Vavi knew that his brother was thinking about him. Their mochas had gone cold, but they continued to sip them anyway.

"Are you okay, Vavi?"

"Yeah, of course, I'm okay," he replied. "I'm even better than ever being here with you."

"You sure?"

"I'm fine."

Vavi flicked his cigarette onto the sidewalk.

"You should quit smoking," Vavi said. "It's bad for you. You know that."

"I know. I will. How about I'll quit when you quit?"

Vavi shook his head. He asked Ravi how he was doing. Ravi told him about Brandi.

"Why don't you ask her out more often?" Vavi asked.

"I will when I'm ready," Ravi said.

"When will you be ready?"

"When I'm happy."

"When will you be happy?"

"When you find a place to live."

"You're depressed," Vavi said. "And I didn't need to go to school to figure this out."

Vavi lit another cigarette and sighed as he blew the smoke from his nostrils.

"You got what sounds like a wonderful, beautiful friend," he continued, "yet you do nothing. You continue to live in your head. Do something."

"Why don't you come to my place? You can sleep there for the night. Just for tonight, you know."

"You don't get it, do you?" Vavi said. "It's not about me. It's about you. Do you know what made Mother and Father so great? They were happy. Even when they were sad or angry or confused, they were deeply happy inside."

"I don't need a lecture."

"This is not a lecture. It's the truth. Listen."

"Why should I listen to you? You're on the streets writing about sea creatures while begging for pennies. You look like a drunken mongrel from hell."

"What, you want to argue?" Vavi asked. "We're not arguing. Look, I'm fine. I'm okay. I've found my place in this world. You? You haven't. You found your place in a world you don't want to be in. I know it. All I do is observe people. Going to work, shopping, talking, shouting, drinking. I see in their eyes what I see in your eyes. The mundane."

He said all this with a smile—a smile full of lies.

"Let's go for a walk," Ravi said. "There's a park nearby."

They took their cups and made their way to the park, which was about a two-minute walk from the coffee shop, located in the middle of a small suburban area. When they arrived at the park, Vavi suggested sitting at the table that had a covering over it to protect it from the rain. It was a red, metallic table, one piece, with the bench connected to the main part. They both didn't sit on the bench but on top of the table itself. Ravi got straight to the point.

"Think about Mother and Father," he said. "Think about their heads against the wall. The blood was everywhere. Think about their broken bodies, their broken brains. Their faces were so smashed up that we couldn't identify them if it weren't for their clothes. Think about it."

"I have."

"No. Think about it."

"I have. That was a long time ago. It's over."

"Think about it. It's not over. Think about it."

"I have. There's nothing to think about."

"Think about it. Don't be a fucking coward. Don't run away. Think about it."

Their talk was over. Vavi pushed Ravi, causing him to fall off the table, and he skidded against a small pad of concrete to which the table was attached so no one could steal it. It was a hard push. His elbows burned from the friction with the concrete. The sleeves of his pink jacket ripped, and he felt the cool air stinging his knees, where his pants had torn, too.

Ravi looked up and saw that Vavi was standing. He got back up and thought that if this was going to be it, then let it be it, and he pushed his brother back and punched him in the stomach. Vavi regained his composure and straightened himself up. His eyes were red, and he was breathing hard. They were both breathing hard. With a grunt, Vavi hit him.

Ravi had already lost the fight. There was no way he could get him back. A strike to his cheek and then to his thigh caused him to fall to the concrete where both their coffee cups had fallen. Ravi smelled the mocha as he closed his eyes and tried to defend himself, but Vavi had put him in a daze. With each hit, he had flashes of pictures of himself hanging in Ghost Town. The hat was still there, and the sun was still setting, giving a beautiful glow onto the horizon. In between hits, he thought of playing Connect Four with Vavi and how all the pieces would come crashing down onto the carpet once the button was pushed at the end of the game.

He was hanging. Vavi. He was hanging. Vavi. He was hanging. Crash. Rope. Connect Four. Beautiful glow. Love you, Vavi. Cowboy hat. Vavi. Ghost Town. Brother. Brother. Vavi. Vavi. Cyclist. Pink. Mother, Father, love you. Vavi, love you. Brandi. Kiss. Brandi. Brother. Love. People. Tyrannosaurus Rex. Stegosaurus. Spikes. Night. Sleep. Sleep. These images and thoughts flowed as Vavi hit him.

The grunting, cursing, and pummeling, stopped. Ravi was still in a daze. His head was ringing, and he could barely breathe. His face was all scraped up, bleeding everywhere, from underneath his eyes to his ankles. He curled up like a roly-poly that had been poked by a finger and let the pain simmer for a few minutes. He wanted to kiss Brandi. He slowly came back to reality.

It was completely silent, but it was hard for him to tell with the ringing in his head. He stood up slowly and rubbed his head and body. He spat blood into the small puddle of spilled mocha. Vavi was crouched over with his arms on his knees as he coughed and breathed loudly. He took out a cigarette from the pack on the table, sat down on the tabletop, and lit it. Ravi limped over to the table and sat down.

Vavi scooted in close to him and put his hand underneath his brother's shirt and pressed against certain spots on his stomach, inspecting Ravi the way a doctor would. Ravi thought about the time they watched *The Karate Kid* together, thinking about when Mr. Miyagi was taking care of Daniel. Then Vavi rubbed his fingertips on the dark shades underneath his brother's eyes, and then he pulled his torn sleeves up and saw the scrapes and blood on his elbows and arms. The stinging caused Ravi's eyes to water. Vavi pulled up his tattered shirt and pressed against his stomach and ribs again, causing Ravi to wince. He tried to hide it, but the pain was too great for him not to grunt. Vavi immediately removed his hand as Ravi whispered a moan.

He looked at his older brother—it was the first time he had seen him cry so hard, so forcefully. It was a deep wail mixed in with a sick man's cough—coming from every cell of his body. From red blood cells and brain cells and skin cells, his tears were born, and they dripped down his cheeks to the dirt on his collar. The spirit in his crying reminded Ravi of the Blues singers from the South, tearing up their souls through their raspy voices and rusty harmonicas. He saw these guys on a documentary once, late at night on TV, and he had never seen or heard anything like it before, until then.

Vavi had one hand on Ravi's shoulder, and he rubbed his forehead with the other. His rusted throat drowned the sounds of the engines, pedestrians, birds, and shaking trees around them, sounding like a crying hyena.

In between his gasps for breath, Vavi repeatedly told him that he was sorry. He sounded like an old man—an old, withered, drowned man. They smoked another cigarette and silently listened to the Seattle noises muffled by the surrounding trees shaking in the wind. It reminded Ravi of his quiet spot near Bruce Lee's grave. The grass had a fresh, dark green color to it. Near the middle, where the ground sunk in a bit, was a small pond, looking more like a large puddle.

Ravi looked at Vavi. He was not the older brother that he used to be. He had become a child who needed help and love. He missed his parents. His senses and his experience, coolness, and maturity from all the years had dwindled with the rise of his loneliness. Ravi, at the same time, was not his younger brother. He was just a child in search of the love he had grown accustomed to years ago. His smile, his laughter—the real smiles, the real laughter—had diminished with the death of his parents and Vavi's departure. They were brothers—no one was younger and no one was older—just brothers who had become lost, and now they were slowly finding themselves, each other. *It feels strange*, Ravi thought. But it also felt nice.

"I didn't handle it properly, did I?" Vavi said.

"I don't blame you. It was rough."

"I should have been there for you."

"Too much to handle."

"I'm sorry."

"There's no need to be sorry," Ravi said. "It was a rough time. I understand. I was there, too. We fell apart after that, but the main thing now is coming back together. That's the main thing, you know."

"You, Mother, and Father are everything to me," Vavi said. "And when they died, I felt like I wasn't a part of this world anymore. Everything was there, but they were all just forms to me, nothing concrete. You all were my life."

"But then you left when you needed to stay," Ravi said. "We could have gone through it together."

Ravi told him about his dreams, his trouble with sleeping, and his proneness of being alone. He told him about feeling numb like he was under anesthetics for the past million years. Vavi was at his limit in vulnerability. He was crying again as Ravi told him about his visions of hanging.

"You really have a rope next to your bed?" Vavi asked.

"I had to. I thought it would help."

"This is no way for us to live."

"I agree."

"I mean," Vavi continued, "all this time I thought I was okay. I thought everything was fine, you know? Did you know that I never really cried about their death? I tried and I tried, but I just couldn't. I was worried. Why can't I grieve? It just built up and built up, and after all these years, it just comes out. Because of you, it comes out."

"Well, you know I know that it was a lot to take. We handle things differently, I know. But it just didn't make sense that we never talked about their death."

Vavi wiped his face with his shirt and got off the table and stretched. He apologized for fighting, and Ravi did the same. Ravi asked him where he was going.

"For a walk," Vavi said.

"So, this is it?" Ravi asked.

"For now."

He had a huge smile on his face, revealing his teeth. Ravi was surprised at how white and clean his teeth appeared.

"Do you brush your teeth?" Ravi asked.

"Every morning and every night," Vavi replied. "Mouthwash. We are the dying dogs."

"What?"

"What that lady said to you in the grocery store. The dogs are us. The strays. She is asking why the strays die. She must be close to her death, I guess."

"Well," Ravi said. "Today was fun."

He wanted to ask Vavi to stay with him at the apartment for the night, but he held back this time.

"The fight wasn't so bad," Ravi said. "I almost had you."

They both laughed.

"We should do it again," Vavi said. "I have a lot to think about. Oh. I'm almost finished with my script, too."

"When are you going to let me read it?"

"When you see it on the big screen" Vavi replied. "It's going to be a good one."

He spoke in a low, confident voice, and Ravi realized how serious he was about it. *Maybe I was wrong*, Ravi thought. Maybe it wasn't some low-scale, B-movie, but a blockbuster instead.

Vavi hugged him and rubbed his head. He picked up his bags. He took three seconds to perform each of these actions, all with a smile—it was like he was savoring each motion. Before he walked away, he asked his younger brother for some money, and Ravi pulled out all that he had, which was a ten-dollar bill. Vavi didn't take it, though.

"Looks like you need that more than I do," Vavi said.

As he walked away, he told his younger brother to stop dreaming and start living. Ravi lit a cigarette. Though battered both physically and mentally, he felt better after the talk with Vavi. He thought that his brother was finally facing reality—that their parents were dead, that they were murdered, and all that was left was them two. He had moved to the streets to live in peace. He had let everything go, all his possessions, Ravi, his aunt, and he chose to live a solitary life on the streets, but Ravi hoped that things would start to change. Ravi thought about himself. He guessed that he needed some closure about the past with his brother, before opening up again to the world. Was it time to start living?

"Steady," he said.

23

Ravi left the park and went back to the apartment to clean himself. The blood and dirt slowly swirled in the drain. It reminded him of the peanut butter and jelly jars sold at the grocery store—the ones where both the peanut butter and the jelly were mixed in one jar. They could be found in Aisle B. He had started to bruise, and the darkened rings around his eyes made him look like a raccoon. As he brushed his teeth, he checked to see if any were loose or lost, but they were all there, sturdy and set.

Brandi had left a message on the answering machine. Before Brandi, he would forget that he even had an answering machine because it had been so long since someone had left a message. He rarely checked the machine, but the blinking red light managed to get his attention. She was going to the movie theater—to a 5:00 showing—and she wanted to know if Ravi would like to join her. Though tired, he decided to meet her. He wasn't used to coming and going all the time, and he hadn't had a good sleep in a while, but the thought of seeing Brandi reenergized him. He lay in bed, passing time by staring at the ceiling until his eyes collapsed. He couldn't sleep, but at least his eyes were closed.

There he was: it was much colder in this vision than the earlier ones. He could smell the friction of the rope rubbing against his neck. Barefoot this time. No shirt. Scars all over his body. Where did these scars come from? He could feel the weather on his back—the sun keeping a dead man warm—something like 80 degrees. The cowboy hat on the wooden boards below inched closer to him as the wind blew, causing it to shuffle about. It was like he was in the middle of the desert. Nothing else around. No buildings, horses, cactuses—nothing. Not even a dust ball rolling around. When he opened his eyes, it was to time meet Brandi.

For a Friday night, the theater was not crowded. He bought one ticket to a romantic comedy and opened the door to the hall. The room was already dark, and the previews had finished. As he surveyed the place, he saw a few groups of people spread around. One person was sitting alone on the opposite side from where he was standing, but he couldn't tell if the person was Brandi. The person turned around to Ravi and waved to him with a lit-up cell phone in hand to help Ravi see.

"Cell phone," he whispered.

He ducked his head and hated himself for walking in front of a group of people who were already sitting. He told them that he was sorry, and they told him to hurry up.

"Brandi," he said.

She turned her head—even in the dark, her smile could kill Ravi. She moved her legs to the side to let him through. She smelled like he wanted to kiss her. As soon as he sat down, she placed her arm around his and put her head on his shoulder. His shoulder was still sore from the fight with his brother, and he tried hard not to wince after a while, he became used to the pain.

They didn't talk to each other at all as the movie played. They barely moved, and she kept her arm under his throughout the whole show. The movie wasn't too good, but Ravi wasn't giving it any attention. His thoughts were with Brandi, her body lotion, and her arm being around his. It was good to be next to her. She laughed now and then along with the rest of the crowd, and Ravi laughed, as well, to make it look like he was really watching the movie. During a sad part, Ravi, with his peripheral vision, could see her turn her head and look at him, and she moved her face close to his and breathed onto his lips. Lip gloss. He couldn't recognize the scent, maybe because of the strawberry body lotion, but he thought it was cherry. He turned his head and looked at her. Her eyes, round and glossy, made him want to dive in them and swim. They kissed. His hand was on her knee. One of her hands tickled his chin while her other hand rubbed his inner thigh. They kissed while the scene changed, and the rest of the crowd was laughing. When the laughter stopped, they stopped kissing.

They didn't talk to each other until after the movie finished. They were standing outside the theater. Her eyes were slightly red from crying at the end of the show when the two main characters resolved their problems and kissed. Brandi had her hair tied in a ponytail, and she was wearing a knee-length maroon skirt, a black long-sleeve shirt, and a pair of dark-red walking shoes. She had on a touch of mascara and pink lipstick. Ravi could picture her in a magazine advertisement for a clothing store. He was in love with someone who had red eyes.

She stared at Ravi and gently glided her hand over his face, over the small cuts and bruises. She blew underneath his eyes.

"Look at you," she said. "You look like a boxer."

She was almost whispering.

"Yeah, but not a very good one."

"What happened?"

"Just talked with my brother not too long ago," Ravi said. "I'll tell you later. Sorry I was late."

"I'm glad you came."

"Coffee?"

"You know it."

They started walking, and Ravi told her about his talk with his brother. She reacted to every sentence with widening eyes, jumping up or down, waving her arms, or putting her hands against her face.

"It's nice," Ravi said. "I feel a lot better now. And I think we both still feel kind of strange. I think more of him than I do. He still won't stay with me. He won't let me help him at all."

They walked into a coffee shop where Brandi spotted some of her friends. They waved to her, motioning for her to come to join them. She grabbed Ravi's hand.

"Just for a few minutes," she said.

Ravi leaned back, trying not to budge, but she yanked his arm, causing him to stumble forward. One of her friends grabbed a chair for her, but not for Ravi.

"Hey," Ravi said, "I'll let you go."

"No," Brandi said. "Stay. Come sit for a bit."

She grabbed a chair and placed it next to her. Ravi sat down and glanced at the people sitting at the table. Brandi introduced him to them, but as always, he didn't remember any of their names. He vaguely recognized a couple of the faces from the last time he ran into Brandi at the café. A thin guy with a thin mustache and long hair tied in a ponytail sat across from him. He inhaled his cigarette and blew the smoke in rings like it was his introduction. Next to him sat the lady with the spiky hair. This time, her hair was dyed bright yellow with black spots spread throughout, resembling the skin of a cheetah or leopard. She didn't look at Ravi, but at Brandi, asking her how she was doing. Next to the cheetah girl sat a guy wearing a black T-shirt and a black baseball cap with no logo—he was playing with a Zippo. He stared at Ravi.

"Who are you?" Zippo asked.

"I just told you," Brandi said. "This is Ravi—a friend of mine. If you weren't stoned all the time, maybe you would remember things."

"I smoke not to remember," he replied, pulling out a cigarette.

Though Ravi had already decided not to like Zippo, he liked the line that the guy had just said—it made him think of Vavi.

"So poetic," Ravi said.

"Speaking of," Ponytail said, "Kelly invited us over. She has some good stuff. Coming?"

Brandi looked at Ravi like he was her parent.

"Oh, I don't care," Ravi said. "Go if you want to, but I don't think I will."

"You weren't invited," Zippo said.

Brandi looked at him and mouthed something with her cheeks sucked in. She was sticking up for Ravi, but Ravi couldn't tell what she was saying. She un-muted her voice and said that she wouldn't be able to go.

"More for us," Ponytail said.

A man and a woman—both covered in gray hair—sat down at the table next to theirs and looked at them. Ravi couldn't tell if the man was grimacing or if that was his normal face, but he could hear his thoughts, saying to himself, *dumb kids, blowing smoke everywhere, showing no respect for their elders, looking like they own the place.* The woman had her hand on his arm, talking, but he wasn't listening. Ravi stood up.

"I think I'm going to go now."

Brandi grabbed his arm.

"Sit," Zippo said.

He kicked Ravi's chair a couple of times. *He must be the leader of the group of friends*, Ravi thought. The one everyone looked up to, sucked up to, and tried to gain his respect.

"Tell me about yourself," Zippo said.

"I really don't have much to say."

He snorted.

"Typical," he said. "You're just an average guy—got nothing to contribute to the world."

Ravi lit a cigarette and remained standing. The old man was still staring at them. Ravi put out his cigarette.

"Well, at least I don't have a Zippo."

Ponytail laughed quietly, looking the other way.

"What's that supposed to mean?" Zippo asked.

"Everything."

As he walked away, something hit the back of his head. It was a coffee cup. Zippo was smiling. Ravi didn't think. He went up to Zippo who was still sitting and put his hand around Zippo's neck, slightly choking him. Nothing was said from either of them. After about five seconds, Ravi pushed him over, causing the chair to fall back, and Zippo hit the table next to him—the table where the old couple was sitting. Ravi walked away, expecting retaliation, but nothing happened. He could hear Brandi say something, and her chair rattled—she caught up to Ravi.

"You want to walk me home?"

They went outside, not saying anything until they reached her house. They held hands the whole time.

"What was that all about?" Brandi asked.

"I don't know. The guy was a jerk."

"You didn't have to push him over like that."

"If you're going to talk trash, you should be ready for a reaction. I couldn't just let him get away with that."

"I thought you didn't care about anything anymore," Brandi said.

Ravi didn't know how to respond, and he stared at her shoes. If he was by himself when that had happened, he probably wouldn't have cared. But it was because of Brandi that he had reacted. She made him care. She hugged him.

"Give me a call some time," she said

"I will."

She looked like she wanted to say something.

"Are you okay?" Ravi asked.

"I'm fine. Why?"

"Just asking,"

"Look," she said. "I know you know I like you, and I know you like me. Why don't we spend more time together and see where this goes?"

"I know," Ravi said. "I do like you. I do want to spend more time with you. A lot more time. But it's kind of strange right now. I don't know if I'm ready."

"You'll know if you're ready if you try."

"I know, but I don't know if there is any other way of saying this, but I'm kind of fucked up in the head."

"Aren't we all?"

She's brilliant, Ravi thought.

"This is different," he said. "I'm not right in the head. And I don't think you can handle it. Really."

"Yeah. Well, try me. You need to be around people. You should learn to trust others. Be with others. I'm here, right in front of you, opening the door, asking you to come in."

"Not that easy," Ravi said.

"Why?"

"Not that easy to answer."

"You want to live your life like a sad and depressed guy, don't you?"

She sounds like Vavi, Ravi thought.

"Your brother is right," Brandi said. "You told me that you told your brother that he's scared. You're scared, too. You're scared of happiness. Open up. You couldn't even spend ten minutes with my friends."

"That's your friends' fault."

Ravi didn't know what else to say. He had told her everything that he wanted to tell her about himself. She knew him more than he knew himself. What else was there to say?

"Maybe I'm wrong," Brandi said. "Maybe I'm picturing something that's not there."

"It's not that. I'm not too good about opening up or spending time with people. What do you want to know? You know about my parents and my brother. That's where I'm coming from."

"I know," Brandi said. "But there's more to it. That can't be your whole life. Like, what do you like to do in your free time? Your favorite food? Movies? Music? Books?"

She raised her hands toward the sky.

"How do you like to end your nights before you sleep? What are your routines in the morning? You know? The small stuff that becomes a part of our DNA structure. You've got so much left of your life—don't let it just drip away."

"Do you really think I want to be like this? Do you really think so? Of course not. It's just not that easy. If it were that easy, we wouldn't be having this conversation at all."

Ravi lit a cigarette.

"Look, Brandi, please stop. Not now. Please."

"Fine."

She turned around and walked up the porch stairs to her door. As she turned the lock with her key, he wanted to say something, but he kept his mouth closed. He wanted to tell her that he was falling in love with her. She didn't look back as she walked in. She didn't slam the door—she closed it gently, and Ravi could hear the lock turning. He didn't leave at first and sat down on the steps, rubbing his forehead.

He wasn't used to having close friends or being around someone daily. He hadn't done that since Vavi had left. He had become too accustomed to a solitary life. Only his thoughts had kept him company, and these thoughts mainly consisted of him hanging himself. Ravi realized how Vavi must have felt when he asked his brother to move in with him. He realized that he, himself, was not ready for that—for being around people. He understood that it wasn't that simple to change his lifestyle, no matter how badly he wanted to change it. He had felt this feeling of anesthesia for the past eight years, and now the liveliest, most beautiful person was standing before him, telling him that she was the cure.

It's an addiction, Ravi thought. Perhaps it was like someone on drugs, wanting to change lifestyles but always going back to it. Ravi didn't know much about drugs, but he wondered if the mentality was the same. The hunger to quit was there, but the food to feed the hunger was not enough to annul the addiction. He wanted to get rid of this loneliness. He saw glimpses of happiness. He wanted to extinguish his daydreams of Ghost Town and spend time with others, especially Vavi and Brandi, but he was too prone to keep to himself, whether he liked it or not.

It started to rain, so he ran to a sheltered bus stop and huddled in with the rest of the crowd as they waited for the bus. He thought of Vavi and wondered if he had found a dry place. When the bus came, the rain changed to a drizzle, and Ravi decided to walk back to the apartment. On the way, he stopped at the grocery store to find some kind of pain reliever. Randy was at the front of the store as he entered.

"What the hell happened to you?" Randy asked.

"Nothing. Just a misunderstanding."

"You okay?"

"I'm alright. Just need some medicine."

"You want an apron, too?" Randy asked. "We could use some help."

"Maybe later. I just need some medicine right now."

"Well. You know where it is. Bring it to me, and I'll give you your employee discount."

Ravi thanked him and walked to the back of the store for some Advil. A strange feeling of nostalgia came over him, which he thought was unusual. He didn't think he would miss working at the grocery store, but the dull and humming lights, Randy, the smell of produce, and the cluttered aisles filled with misplaced items all made him feel remorseful for leaving the place. The store was always good to him. It helped him keep his mind off things. It allowed him to be around people, and at the same time, he was still able to keep his distance and sustain his solitude.

Back at the apartment, Ravi stared into the mirror before swallowing a couple of pills. He saw decay: skin thinning; eyes worn and surrounded by black sandbags underneath; thin wrists; frequent vomiting and coughing. His ribs stuck out, and his stomach was bloated with gas and emptiness—coffee and cigarettes were not a steady diet. The acidity bubbled inside every time he tried to eat chips or Ramen. Mother would have told him to eat more yogurt.

Someone knocked on his door, and Ravi stood as still as if he had just been caught in a game of freeze tag. The tap on the door came again. Ravi stood in the bathroom, contemplating whether he should open the door or not. The person on the other end called his name—a female voice. She knew his name. *Brandi? Or maybe it's the girl in the next apartment,* he thought.

He walked quietly into the living room, avoiding the creaky spots on the wooden floor, and he made sure not to bump into the coffee table. Again, he stopped as if he had just been tagged. Another knock, and she called his name. The last knock won him over, and he opened the door and saw Annie in a dark green skirt and a black top. She still had the bracelets around her wrist. Ravi didn't say anything, but he looked at her feet—she was wearing sandals. Her toenails were painted bright orange, matching her fingernails. Black eyeliner. Red lipstick. Her cheeks were lightly powdered.

"You look horrible," she said.

"Hey."

"How's it going?" she asked.

"No one has ever knocked on my door. This is strange."

"Usually what happens next is that you ask me to come in."

"Come in."

"I mean, if that's okay," Annie said. "I don't mean to barge in or anything. Just thought I'd come in and say hi."

Neither of them moved.

"How did you know where I live?"

"Randy told me. I just came from the grocery store."

"When did you get in?"

"Yesterday."

They remained standing in the doorway.

"Sorry about taking off like that," she said.

"You had me worried for a while. But no need to be sorry."

He was looking at her ankles most of the time, only glancing at her eyes whenever she spoke.

"How are you doing?" Ravi asked.

"I love New York. It's the place I needed to be. I'm thinking of moving there."

"Wow. That's great."

"You don't sound like you think it's great."

"It's great."

"And I'm seeing this nice guy—his name is Thomas. We met at some clothing store. He's a sweet guy. Reminds me of you."

She's talking much faster than before, Ravi thought. He looked at the floor and counted the carpeted squares. Annie sat down on the floor and leaned her back against the edge of the doorway. Ravi sat down with her.

"How've you been?" Annie asked. "We should exchange phone numbers and email addresses and keep in touch."

"Yeah, we should. I'm doing okay. Not really working anymore, and I've been talking to someone."

"Oh yeah?"

"Yeah. She's really nice. Sweet."

"Well," Annie said. "Good luck with that. You deserve it. You're a great guy."

She stood up and stuck her hand out to help Ravi get back up onto his feet.

"What happened to your face?"

"I got in a fight with my brother. We're okay now. Just a simple misunderstanding."

"Just a simple misunderstanding? It looks more complicated than that."

Annie took out a piece of paper and a pen and wrote down her contact information. She tore the paper in half so that Ravi could write down his information.

"Great," she said. "I felt horrible for leaving without saying bye, but I knew I was going to come back. And I thought I would get your number when I came back."

"Well, I'm glad you did."

"How are your dreams?"

Ravi didn't answer, and she nodded her head. She hugged him and stood on her toes to kiss him on the top of his head.

"Keep in touch," she said.

After Annie left, Ravi didn't bother with lying in bed. He checked into a hotel a couple of blocks down. It was a small hotel, consisting of two floors. They served continental breakfast in the morning, and other than that, they had bagels and sandwiches for the rest of the day. They didn't have a pool—not that he would have gone swimming, anyway—just a small outside patio with wooden chairs and tables. Room 154 was where he stayed—all the way in the back of the hotel. He kept one lamp on, and he turned the television on to the weather channel and muted it.

Ravi loved the way hotel beds were made with their bedsheets tightly tucked under the mattress. He tugged on the sheets just enough to where he could slide through, keeping the blankets as kempt as possible. He stared at the ceiling. Stared and stared. He counted all the flecks and bumps of plaster—a universe of its own. It was a microcosm of his brain, and it was the epitome of nothing. Ravi made shapes out of the dots like they were clouds. Dinosaurs, mainly. *When will my brain give out? When will I sleep for a million years? When will Vavi smile forever? When will I let go? When will Brandi understand? When will I understand?*

24

For the first time, Ravi called someone to meet him at the coffee shop—Annie. She sounded surprised to hear his voice on the other line. Ravi's voice wavered on the phone, nervous for some reason like he was a thirteen-year-old asking someone out on a first date.

But once they met at the café, all was fine—Ravi lost his nervousness. It was like she had never left. She spoke loudly, moving her arms, laughing, and touching him on the arm. She was more confident and energetic, keeping her chest raised—crossing her legs and uncrossing them. Her voice bounced around the room. She was in love. She would like to stay in New York to be with her boyfriend.

"So, you ended up with a Marketing guy? He sold you his body, and you bought it?"

"Shut up," Annie said. "He's a nice guy. He tells me every day about how much he loves me. He cooks for me, and we go for walks. I'm just having a blast. What about you? How's it going with your new friend?"

"Okay, I guess. I don't think I'm really giving her what she's looking for."

"And what's that?"

"I guess what your boyfriend gives to you."

"Do you like her?" Annie asked.

"A lot."

"Then why don't you go for it?"

"I don't know."

"Well, if you like her and don't do anything about it, then you're cheating yourself and her."

As Annie finished her sentence, she looked up and saw someone standing behind Ravi. He turned around and saw

Brandi—he asked her to pull up a chair, introducing the two to each other.

"I've been calling you," Brandi said. "Why don't you ever pick up or call me back?"

"Sorry," Ravi said.

"So, this is the Annie you've been talking about," Brandi said.

"You've been talking about me?" Annie asked.

"Yes," Brandi said. "Don't worry—all good things. It's really nice to meet you."

Brandi looked away.

"Well, we were just talking about you," Annie said.

Brandi didn't say anything. Ravi's knees started shaking, and he fidgeted around.

"I hadn't seen Ravi in a while, and he gave me a call today, so we decided to meet up."

"He called you?" Brandi asked.

Annie nodded and looked at Ravi.

"Well, you must be special, because he has never called me before. You know what, let me leave you two alone. I don't want to intrude."

Brandi started to get up.

"Please stay," Ravi said.

"I guess I'll see you later," Brandi said.

She walked off.

"Go after her," Annie said.

Ravi didn't move.

"Come on, man, go after her. She's asking for you by walking away."

"I wish," he said.

Annie sat back and cleared her throat.

"Well," Annie said. "You should go after her. Let her know that you care for her."

"It's not that easy."

"Why?"

"Not ready."

"You don't have to be ready. You don't need to practice it or anything. Look, you and I are the same—were the same. We lived lonely lives. We were the loneliest people, wanting to be alone. But it's dumb."

"But if that's the way I am, what's wrong with that?"

"Nothing. Everything. But come on, really, I saw the glow in your eyes when she walked in. That's not the look of wanting to be alone. That's the look of silent awe."

She's right, Ravi thought. They sat silently, staring at the table and each other's hands for a few seconds. Ravi started talking about movies, asking her if she had seen anything lately. She talked about the indie movies she had seen in New York—in a theater where they served pizza and beer. Ravi moved on to the past—when they used to work at the grocery store together. He felt like he was at a high school reunion. It was weird to him—he and Annie never really hung out a lot, but sitting there with her and talking about the past brought on a sense of nostalgia.

They talked for another half hour until she said she had to go. They hugged, and Annie told her to call him some time so that they could meet up again. Annie looked at him with a slight grin.

"Don't be afraid," she said.

She waved and walked out of the coffee shop. Ravi listened to her sandals clapping against the floor as she left.

25

"Always remember where you come from," Vavi had said one day.

His wobbly head searched for something to lean on. He stumbled across the room and flopped onto his bed as he took off his shirt, revealing the thin gold chain with the Om emblem around his neck. He didn't look at Ravi but stared at his wrists, instead.

"Remember. We are Bengalis—we're from India. Our family is from the East. We are most spiritual when we are not—when we don't know it."

Vavi burped and rubbed his stomach.

Ravi had no clue what he was talking about and assumed that he must have gotten it from one of the books he had read. Vavi took a long sip from his bottle and threw it in the trash can. Ravi didn't want his parents to see it, so he took it out and hid it in his room until he could find the right time to throw it away in secrecy.

Ravi thought about that moment as he approached his brother—he was sitting down on the sidewalk and leaning against the coffee shop.

"What a waste," Vavi said.

"What do you mean?"

"You know what I mean. What a waste."

As Ravi stood in front of the café, looking down at his half-gone older brother, he thought about that first time he had caught Vavi drinking in his room late at night, and he realized now that Vavi was talking about himself—he was calling himself a waste.

He gave his older brother a slight nudge to see if he was awake. His head barely lifted, just enough to see Ravi's face.

"What?" Vavi asked.

"You okay?"

"Of course."

"You don't look it."

"Shut up. Leave me alone."

"Why don't you get up for a bit?"

Ravi tried pulling on his arm, but he resisted just as much.

"Mother and Father would have been proud of me," Vavi said.

He grunted and pushed his knee.

"I'm no sunflower now," Vavi said.

"I still look up to you."

Vavi tried to get up, holding onto the wall behind him for guidance, but he fell back down.

"Leave me alone," Vavi said.

He took a sip from whatever bottle was inside a brown lunch bag. Ravi tried to take it out of his hand, but Vavi pushed his knee away again, and Ravi couldn't keep his balance. He fell backward. A few pedestrians looked at Ravi, but none offered to help him up. He wondered if they thought that he was homeless, too, with his stained and torn pink jacket and his bruised and tired face. Vavi didn't say anything. Ravi got up and walked away without saying anything, rubbing his lower back, and feeling the scrapes on his skin through his shirt.

"It's going to be the greatest jellyfish ever," Vavi said.

Ravi kept walking.

At the bar—the same one where Ravi had met Brandi for the first time—he sat by himself in the corner. It was not as crowded as his last visit and much darker than before—it wasn't a dancing night. Groups consisting of a few people outlined the walls, and Ravi was the only one sitting at the bar.

He ordered a whiskey. The first sip brought back the memory of sitting at some broken-down bar, drinking glass after glass by himself until the bartender had kicked him out—it wasn't near closing time either. He had arrived around five for happy hour, and he didn't leave until around midnight. He remembered that, while walking home, he had found some alley and crept through the darkness to vomit as quietly as possible. The sides of the building, the dumpster, and the people staring had all spun around him. The flies were the only ones that had stayed in place.

Brandi sat on the barstool next to him, not saying hi.

"Can I get you a drink?" Ravi asked.

"No."

She ordered a gin and tonic.

"Another one for me, please—extra shot," Ravi said.

They sat silently like they didn't know that the other person was there, ordering drink after drink, and the neon lights gradually turned into neon splotches.

"What's your problem?" Ravi asked.

"What's your problem?" she asked back.

They both took a sip of their drinks.

"Don't be a jerk," she said.

"You too."

"Why don't you call me like you called Annie?"

"None of your business."

"Fuck you."

Ravi couldn't say that back.

"It's nothing," Ravi said. "Really."

She took out her cell phone and plopped it into her drink.

"Why'd you do that?"

"It's not like I need it."

"You're overdoing it."

"And you're not doing anything."

"I just wanted to catch up with her," Ravi said.

"That's fine," Brandi said. "That's not the point. My point is that you never call me. You never ask me to do anything, yet you call everyone else."

"Yeah, right—everyone else," Ravi said sarcastically.

Ravi was too drunk to have any patience.

"Do you like me?" she asked.

Too direct.

"Do you want to be with me?"

Ravi opened his mouth like he was about to say something, but he took another sip instead.

"Fuck you," Brandi said.

She ordered a drink for Ravi, telling the bartender that Ravi was going to need it because he was going to live the rest of his life alone and he needed to drink more so he could forget his miserable life. She stood up and walked away, not saying bye. Ravi was glad that she walked away first because he was going to need a couple more hours to stay drunk.

26

Was this really happening? Was Brandi real? He had touched her skin and kissed her lips, but was it all real? Did his brother beat him down? Was Vavi living on the streets? Ravi thought that Vavi was going to get better after their last talk, but he just fell back down again. Where were his parents? Were they really dead? Why? Why anything? Why nothing?

Reality had become a dream. Life had become unreal. Was he hanging with a cowboy hat placed below his feet, or were his raccoon eyes and broken body real? Ravi found himself caught in a blend—a mixture of reality and dream. But was it real? And was reality just a quest for normality or stability? He asked himself these questions but didn't even bother to answer them. He knew he wanted to kiss Brandi again, and he knew he wanted to be around Vavi, but where did all that fit into the blend? Those small bubbles that formed in the foam after a wave crashes—that was what Ravi felt like. In a world full of oceans of people, he found himself in the foam, covered in salt and surrounded by drifting seaweed.

As he sat in the cemetery and gazed at Bruce Lee's grave, he rubbed his hand over the swollen spots on his face and let the environment take over. There was a breeze. There was always a breeze at the cemetery. It caressed the back of his neck, and it soothed his battered brain—it tickled. The wind caused the bushes to shake, making the sound of a waterfall falling miles away. Along with the sound of the distant waterfall, Ravi could faintly hear traffic. The sun was there too, and it gave warmth to his back. It made him feel like he was floating on warm water in a hotel swimming pool. It was all meshed. It was all mixed, blended, interwoven, and attached. He almost fit in. Almost. *Maybe I would feel in place if Brandi and Vavi were around*, he thought. That would have made it a perfect nature, a perfect system.

He let himself float on the warm water that tickled his back. He thought about Ghost Town. Ravi tried to fight it. He closed his eyes, hard, like a clenched fist, like he was trying to move matter with his mind. He tried to visualize a rainbow, a bright one, flashing and glittering, illuminating the gray sky. Ravi pictured a swimming pool underneath it, full of those foam noodles floating around, kids jumping in, shouting and laughing. Some ate blue snow cones—the bubblegum flavor—and others ate green ones—that was the watermelon flavor. There were yellow ones—banana flavored—and red ones—strawberry. Some had all the colors mixed into one. Ravi tried to think about tennis— Pete Sampras playing against Andre Agassi in the U.S. Open, going to the full 5 sets with tiebreakers in the last two, the audience with mouths opened wide, clapping, sitting and standing, sitting and standing. He moved on to thinking about Brandi, naked, taking a shower, washing with a sponge, scraping it along her skin, her thighs, and her stomach. Ravi started rubbing his thighs, gradually making his way to his zipper, to grasp sensuality, to forget about everything else.

It didn't work. His hands were tied behind his back. His legs dangled in the wind, causing the wooden platform to creak—a quiet creak, almost soporific, like the tides at night. The cowboy hat was made of steel—it sat underneath his legs. The rope burned as the friction increased from the swaying in the gusts. It burned so much that his neck caught fire—a perfect ring, melting his skin away, exposing his collarbone and vertebrae. Ravi opened his eyes, and he was still there—nowhere else but there.

He felt something splatter on the back of his neck and his shoulder, startling him and taking him out of his dream. Bird excrement—brown and white and warm. He didn't wipe it. He let it stay there. *That was real*, Ravi told himself. This was real. He looked up, and through the branches covered in thick, bright, yellow-green leaves, he saw a brown bird hopping along. He told the bird thanks. He waved to it, telling it to come to him. He wanted to kiss that bird.

27

Brandi left a message for him on the answering machine, asking him to go meet her at a coffee shop he had never been to before—The Brewery. It wasn't too far from where he lived, and he walked there. He thought about what he was going to say when he saw her. He thought that this was going to be one of those talks—one of talks where they let it all out. He didn't have much to say to her, though. It was only a few words—that he needed her.

As he walked into the coffee shop, he saw Brandi and a couple of other people sitting in some lounge chairs in the corner of the café. The other two people were Ponytail and Zippo, but the spiky-haired girl wasn't there. He immediately understood that this would not be the visit he was expecting—that maybe she was setting him up for something. He stopped and pretended not to see them at first, squinting his eyes, surveying the crowd. Brandi shouted his name, which he could barely hear because the place was full of people, causing a loud hubbub to swirl around the room. When he walked up, Brandi glanced at him and stood up. Ravi opened his arms to hug her, but she walked past him and sat in the same chair as Zippo. One of her legs rested on top of his. Ravi sat down.

She didn't say anything to Ravi and continued to talk to Zippo and Ponytail. It was as if Ravi wasn't there. Ravi wished he wasn't there. He had no clue what they were talking about—something about art, art theory, using long, multi-syllabic words, and they were mentioning names he didn't recognize. He tried not to look at Brandi as she twirled Zippo's hair, rubbing his cheek with the back of her hand, but he caught some glances every now and then.

"Brandi."

She pretended not to hear him.

"Brandi."

None of them look at him. Ravi got up and walked away.

28

A week had passed since Ravi had last seen Vavi, and then he found his older brother sitting outside Beans, slumped against the wall as if hadn't moved one bit since last the last time they had met. Seeing him there that morning made Ravi think of that time when Vavi was taking alcohol to school.

"You're drinking on campus?" Ravi had asked.

"Kind of," Vavi had replied vaguely.

He took some textbooks out of his schoolbag and put a small bottle of Vodka inside. He stuffed a couple of shirts inside the bag so that the bottle wouldn't break, and then he put his textbooks back into the bag.

"You can really get in trouble for doing that, and I'm not talking about school. I'm talking about Father."

"He won't know," Vavi had said. "Just don't say anything, right? I found a nice little hiding spot during break. Just a couple of sips to ease the day. Don't ever let me catch you doing this, okay? "

"Okay."

But in all his memories, Ravi had never seen his brother as totally inebriated as he was now. Vavi was past drunk. His eyes were stitched closed, and his head rocked left to right, never finding balance. His legs were strewn about, lifeless, one hand barely holding a beer bottle while the other hand rested on his lap. He mumbled to the people walking by, telling them about happiness, about finding themselves and not giving in to the pressures of the world. He lifted one leg, trying to trip one pedestrian, but while doing so, he knocked over his bottle, causing him to shout curse words. The guy who Vavi was trying to trip looked at him and kicked his leg a couple of times.

"Hey," Ravi shouted. "Hey."

He ran up to the person and gave him a slight push on the back.

"Don't kick him," Ravi said. "Stop that."

The guy just shrugged his shoulders and continued walking, and Ravi turned around and went back to Vavi who was now talking to himself, mumbling about jellyfish and how he hated talk shows. He always hated talk shows. Once, they were sitting in the living room watching some talk show that helped people out with their problems, and without saying anything, Vavi took the remote control out of Ravi's hand and changed the channel. He got up and left. Ravi never knew why he didn't like those kinds of shows, but Ravi never watched them again.

"Vavi. Vavi, it's me, Ravi, your brother."

Beer stained his clothes, and a soft pack of crushed cigarettes poked out of his shirt pocket.

"Spare some change?" Vavi asked. "Give me some money. I need to eat something so it can go into my stomach. Beer. Buy me a beer. I can just drink that and forget about eating. Come on now, give me some money."

Ravi lifted his head and felt blood on the back of it—he had fallen and knocked his head against the side of the coffee shop.

"Vavi, you're hurt—let me clean you up."

Ravi tried to lift him, but Vavi's body didn't move. Everything was limp, and he made no effort to get up. He pushed Ravi away and told him to fuck off.

"Vavi. Come on. Let's go."

"Leave the guy alone," one pedestrian said, walking by.

"Shut up," Vavi said. "All of you shut the fuck up. You don't know. You don't know anything. This world is nothing, and you all are just idiots."

Just hearing him speak made Ravi feel a bit better, but the blood still worried him.

He tried to stand up on his own as he lectured the world, but his arms gave out, causing him to knock his head again against the wall. Ravi could barely look at him. Vavi spat all over himself.

"This is how you bathe," Vavi said. "Mother used to lick her thumb and wipe the dirt off my face."

Ravi's eyebrow rose.

"Right, remember mother? Remember our parents?"

"Fuck yes, I do. Who the fuck are you? Don't ask me about my parents. I know my parents. I loved them. I fucking loved them, and they loved me. My father—my father was the best. He would hold my hands when we walked in the park. Who are you to ask me about my parents?"

"I'm your brother."

"Ravi is my brother," Vavi said. "He's not here. He lives in another world, fucked up like me, and it's all my fault. Jellyfish."

Ravi told him that it wasn't his fault. Vavi shook his head and started knocking the bottle against the ground until it finally broke, cutting his fingers and palm. Blood rushed out in strings, dripping onto the sidewalk. He wiped his hand against his shirt. One of the Beans employees walked outside—he rubbed his face and looked at Vavi.

"I can't believe I have to say this, man," he said, "but you're going to have to get out of here, or I'm going to have to call the police."

"Wait," Ravi said. "Don't call the police. I'll get him out of here. Could you do me a big favor and call a cab for me, though?"

"Sure," he said. "Who are you?"

"Ravi, his brother."

He looked at Ravi with wide eyes and smiled.

"Ah, yes, Ravi. So nice to finally meet you. Vavi has told me a lot about you. A lot of wonderful things about you. It's good that you're here—I don't know what's wrong with him. Never seen him like this before as long as I've been here. Nice to meet you."

He stuck out his hand, and Ravi shook it.

"I'll go inside and get a taxi for you," the employee said. "Oh, and hold on, before I forget."

The guy rushed back inside and came back out holding a stack of paper.

"It's his manuscript. I keep it inside for him so the wind doesn't take it away."

"Thanks," Ravi said. "Where's his bag?"

"I don't know. It's not inside. But anyway, let me get that taxi for you."

"Vavi, where is your bag?" Ravi asked.

His eyes were barely open, and Ravi hoped that he would pass out soon so he wouldn't have to worry about his drunken antics. He thought about getting Vavi another beer, but he didn't want to leave him alone. The barista came back outside and told Ravi that a taxi was coming. Ravi thanked him for his help and apologized.

"Take care of him," he said. "He loves you."

Ravi followed the barista into the coffee shop, took a stack of napkins from the condiment stand, and ran back outside. He wrapped the napkins around Vavi's hand, but the napkin wouldn't stick, so Ravi took off his pink coat and wrapped it tightly around Vavi's hand and arm. He sat next to his older brother, waiting for the taxi, and as he propped his head against the wall, he closed his eyes and saw himself in Ghost Town.

The rope was on fire, but it wasn't burning his skin. It was nighttime, and along with the fire, the blurry stars lit his vision, reminding him of some kind of messed-up Van Gogh painting. In this dream, Ravi was coughing, and his hands were tied behind his back. His socks were red with blood, and the cowboy hat shifted about in the wind.

"If only," he whispered.

His eyes opened to the sound of the taxi honking. A couple of quarters were thrown at Ravi's feet by a pedestrian who thought they both were beggars.

"Shut up," Vavi shouted to the taxi driver. "Please be quiet. We're in a library. Can't you see?"

Ravi got up and ran to the taxi.

"I'm going to need your help and patience," Ravi said. "Extra, extra tip."

"It better be," the driver said

"Just give me a few minutes."

Ravi went back to Vavi and asked him to get up, lifting his head and his arms. Both fell as soon as Ravi let go. He crouched down, cleared his throat, and started speaking Bengali in a faint voice.

"Vavi," Ravi said. "Vavi, listen to me. Listen to your Father now."

He had to think before he said each word, as his Bengali wasn't too fluent. Vavi knew the language quite well— enough to get around Kolkata if he had to. Vavi placed his hands against each side of his head and lifted it straight, away from the wall.

"Vavi, listen to me. Listen to Father. It's time to go. It's time to go home so that you can sleep. Mother is waiting to tuck you in. Come."

Vavi lifted his hand, the one wrapped in his jacket, and placed it against the side of Ravi's face in an endearing manner. just as their mother used to do to them.

"Help me up, Father," he said.

He spoke in slurred Bengali. Ravi turned around and

motioned for the driver to help him.

"What a mess," the driver said.

"He'll be okay," Ravi said.

The driver took one arm and placed it around his shoulder while Ravi did the same with the other arm, and they both grunted as they lifted him, half-dragging him to the taxi. Vavi got into the back and lay down on the seat. Ravi sat in the front and gave the address to his aunt's house.

By the time they arrived at her house, Vavi had passed out, snoring, and drooling over himself.

Ravi ran to the door and rang the bell. Auntie opened the door, dressed in a purple gown. At first, she smiled and said Ravi's name with joy, but when she understood the look on his face, her face changed to a look of concern.

"Vavi," she whispered.

Ravi told her to grab her purse and that he needed her help.

For a woman in her sixties, thin and frail, she surprised Ravi with her strength as they carried Vavi into the house. She grunted and breathed loudly as they took him into the guest bedroom which used to be Ravi's room. Auntie ran off and came back with a wet towel, rubbing alcohol, bandages, and cotton. She unwrapped Vavi's hand and started cleaning it with delicate movements like she had been a nurse all her life. Her hair, pure gray, came down to her shoulders, and her black eyes had not aged—they were still soft and welcoming.

Ravi looked around the room. Because he had taken many of his belongings to his apartment or boxed them up, his bedroom had completely changed its look. Photographs of nature scenes lined the walls. The wooden dresser and the bedside table were bare. There was nothing else there. The room looked completely different from when Ravi used to live in it: thrown-about toys, a shelf—half full of books, half full of trinkets he had received as gifts from his parents—old Bollywood movie posters, and a stereo used to occupy the room.

Vavi opened his eyes for a few seconds and saw Auntie and Ravi peering over them.

"Hi Auntie," Vavi said. "I'm tired. I'm going to sleep."

He closed his eyes, leaving his hand to be tended to.

Auntie knew of Vavi's living conditions, but she never protested it. Once Ravi asked her why, and she had said, in a calm and confident voice, "Because he will find his way eventually."

Ravi explained to her what had happened earlier and why Vavi was in such a condition, and she started talking to herself in Bengali. After she finished wrapping his hand with a roll of brown athletic bandages, she told Ravi that he could sleep in Vavi's old room. Ravi accepted her offer and kissed her on the cheek. She smelled like Mother.

Vavi's room looked exactly the same. Shelves full of philosophy, literature, and psychology books against each wall. On his bedside table, next to the lamp, was a picture of their family in a silver frame. He pictured Vavi in bed, underneath the blanket, reading while sipping Vodka. Ravi lay down on the bed and stared at the ceiling fan for about an hour and a half. He heard Auntie turning off the lights and setting the alarm—a sign that she was soon about to go to bed.

He cracked open the door and saw that all the lights were off. He took off his shoes so that they wouldn't make any noise and walked to the garage where he found what looked like a castle of boxes stacked one on top of another. He thought about looking through them, visiting the past through T-shirts, toys, pictures, compact discs, music cassette tapes, and movies, but he kept his hands in his pockets and walked around the maze of cardboard boxes, smelling the history instead. It smelled like insecticide.

He went back to Vavi's room and paced around, looking at his books, staring at the carpet, until he finally sat down, rubbing his knees. Before leaving the house in the middle of the night, he left Auntie a letter. He wrote in cursive and felt like a second grader:

Dear Auntie,

Thank you so much for taking care of Vavi. As we both know, he has been through a rough time, as we all have. You know, I would also like to apologize for being so distant since I moved out. So many times, I wanted to call you and see how you were doing. So many times, I wanted to drop by with a bag of oranges and a bouquet. So many times, I just wanted to let you know that not a day goes by without me thinking about you. I wish I could have handled everything better, like you. Mother always looked up to you, and so do I. I hope you are well, and I'm sorry I couldn't stay the night. I'll call you soon to see how you and Vavi are doing. Please take care of him. Feed him. Love him. Talk to him.

I love you so much,

Ravi.

He left the letter on the kitchen table and went back to his old room to kiss Vavi on the forehead. *Too late to take the bus,* he thought, so he walked a couple of blocks to a small shopping mall and used the payphone to call for a taxi. It was the same payphone he and Vavi would use to call home. Whenever they would ask their parents to come to pick them up after looking around the toy and comic book store. Sometimes Auntie would go pick them up, and they would stay at her place until their parents could go and get them.

29

It had been a few weeks since he had seen Vavi or Brandi, and during those twenty or so days, Ravi had stayed at his apartment, reading and watching television. He was still taking Advil, and his smoking had increased to about half a pack more each day. He would usually go outside to smoke, but during those few weeks, he stayed in his apartment and blew the smoke out the window. He had picked up one of the books that Brandi had talked about when they had their first meeting at the coffee shop. He liked it and would love to talk to her about it.

Despite wanting to talk to Brandi, Ravi kept to himself. Despite wanting to do a lot of things, Ravi kept to himself. Brandi had called a few times and left messages on the answering machine, but he didn't return her calls. Every time the phone rang, he put his hand on the receiver, wanting to lift it, wanting to apologize for everything, wanting to say *hi, come meet me at the café, or the movie theater*, but he just let it ring until the machine picked it up. He just wanted to be silent for now.

He had been keeping in touch with his aunt, more than he had over the past six years. He called her the day after he left the house, telling her that he couldn't sleep, so he had decided to go back to the apartment to read. She told him that he was always welcome to stay at her house. He asked her about Vavi, and she said that he woke up the next morning, embarrassed, ashamed, and remorseful. He had been in and out of the house since then, sometimes sleeping on the streets, other times on the floor in his room, still trying to get used to domestication. She threw out all the alcohol so that Vavi couldn't take any, and Vavi had made a promise to cut out drinking, putting himself on his own kind of detoxification program. The last time Ravi had talked to her, he told her that he loved her repeatedly, and he had apologized for not keeping in touch with her as often as he should. She was understanding and said that she loved him and that he should go over for dinner one night. A family dinner.

The weather lady had been, for the most part, right with her forecasts. Ravi liked her. She was new. Mr. Thomas, the former meteorologist, had left the news station to pursue another field, so said the other news anchors. Ms. Locksley was always smiling, even when the forecast was cloudy and rainy. She didn't have the same tone of voice as the other news anchors did, but her soft tone kept Ravi's attention. She spoke like she wasn't lecturing, but like she was in the middle of a conversation. She gave the weather a bright tint.

30

At the grocery store, Ravi saw Randy standing in the front, putting up a large display sign for the sale on bread—buy 2, get the third half off. He asked Randy if he needed any help—this was Ravi's way of asking for help.

"Just for tonight," Ravi said. "I'll load up half the aisles. I don't want the pay. I just want to work the aisles."

Randy gave him the shift, and despite Ravi's protest, he would be on the clock—Randy hadn't taken him off the employment list.

Ravi heard the buzzing ceiling lights. Recognizing the few customers in the store, he could make out that it was about midnight. He walked past the vegetables and took a deep breath, breathing in the greens and yellows. He stared at the flower department with its lights out, but the roses were still glowing to him—a reminder of when he and Annie had kissed. A customer—a teenage guy with short black hair and black eyes with his collared shirt tucked into his jeans, came up to him and asked for condoms. The guy scratched his head and didn't look Ravi in the eyes when he spoke. Ravi walked to the hygiene section and showed him the selection that they had.

"Extra large," the guy said.

"Just look. They have the sizes on the front."

He looked from side to side to see if anyone else was walking by.

"Thanks, man."

"Your first time?" Ravi asked.

He spoke as if he had slept with a million people.

"No way, man."

Ravi walked away to let him decide alone.

He felt his heart rate increase and his stomach churn as he saw a lady walk in—she looked like Brandi. She was giggling, talking on the phone, and walking straight to the cookie aisle. Ravi ran to the back of the store and dry gagged, hoping that no one heard him, and then he lost it. He took whatever was in front of him—yogurt containers, milk, orange-juice cartons—and threw them all over the place. He knocked over the display shelf of the maple syrup on sale and kicked the cheese stand, causing it to turn over, spilling the packets of cheese onto the floor. Randy came up from behind him and pinned him against the wall, shouting his name. Ravi barely gained his senses, as flashes of Randy's face and himself hanging flickered in and out of his vision.

"Get out of here," Randy said. "Get out of here now."

Ravi pushed him off and walked back to his apartment. On his way out, the lady who looked like Brandi asked him where she could find some Tylenol. Ravi told her to go fuck herself.

Looking through the window of his kitchen, he saw three young girls playing in the parking lot. They looked like they were around twelve, maybe thirteen, dressed in their pajamas and tennis shoes. The girls must have snuck out—their parents snoring or enjoying the time to themselves while their children were trying to find themselves in a world full of thumbtacks and needles. They were jumping rope, two girls on each end, each with a cigarette, and one hopped in the middle, singing a song. Jump rope. Some guy wearing a long, dark overcoat walked up to them. He was stumbling, and he asked them something. The girls shouted and ran away.

It was two in the morning when there was a knock at the door, and Ravi immediately recognized Brandi's voice calling his name. She didn't stop knocking and repeatedly said his name. Ravi opened the door and saw Brandi—mascara ran down her face, and he could barely see her eyes. Even when she was fucked up, she was pretty—shiny red lips mixed with sorrow. She didn't wait for Ravi to speak and managed to walk into the apartment, sitting down on the couch in the living room. Other than Annie, it was the first time anyone had sat down in his apartment. She sobbed and said his name and told Ravi that she was sorry for everything. Ravi said he was sorry, as well.

He got a roll of toilet paper from the bathroom and handed it to her, waiting for her to calm down. He sat down beside her, his hand rubbing her back. She turned her head and looked at him, right before vomiting on the floor. It all came out in three spasms—all liquid. She mumbled something about taking Valium and liquor. With the same roll of toilet paper, he started soaking up the waste on the floor. Brandi repeatedly told him she was sorry, her eyes only half-opened. He left the toilet paper on the floor and sat down beside her again and asked her what happened.

"I was at my ex's house. You know, the one I told you about. And I wasn't thinking and took some Valium while I was drinking. So dumb."

Her crying turned into a series of coughs, leading to another spasm of vomit. Ravi didn't clean it up and continued to rub Brandi's back.

"He's such a fuck," Brandi said. "He's such a fuck. He was so mean to me, I wished you were there Ravi. I wished you were there so badly."

"What happened?"

"He started calling me all these horrible things. He just goes on and on and laughs with his friends at me."

"Why do you still hang out with him then?"

"I don't what else to do," Brandi said. "I just don't know what else to do. I can't pull away from him. I just think about all the good times we've had, and then I miss him, so I go over to his house. And when I saw you with Annie, I just got so frustrated."

"Every time you want to go over there, just come get me. That guy is no good for you. You deserve someone who cares for you."

"Like you," Brandi said.

"Like me."

Ravi lit a cigarette.

"Look, I wanted to tell you that nothing is going on between me and Annie. We were just catching up."

"I know. But you called her. Do you know how long I've been wanting you to call me? It may sound stupid, but these things matter."

"I'm sorry. I know. I didn't mean to hurt your feelings."

"I'm so sorry about the floor," she said.

"Don't worry about that. You okay?"

"And about the other day," Brandi said. "That was all so stupid. Who am I to force you to rip your ribcage apart for me? And I'm sorry for ignoring you."

"But you're right, though," Ravi said. "I'm falling for you. I realized this when I saw you twirling that guy's hair. That really got to me."

Apart from his family, he had never told anyone how he felt about them. He was glad to be able to let his thoughts out. It was a relief—a released burden. She must be someone he loved because he told her to her face. He told her the truth. Brandi grabbed his hand and rubbed his knuckles.

"You think I'm fucked up, don't you?" she asked.

"I need you."

"I'm on drugs," she said. "I do a lot of drugs. No one really knows except for my ex."

"You make me smile."

Ravi rubbed her knuckles.

"Looks like we both got problems facing the world."

"Everyone does. It's just how you handle it."

"I've done it all," she said. "Since I was thirteen. And there really is no reason why. I have a great family. I'm in a great situation, yet I just want to fuck it all up. It's time for a change."

Ravi placed his hands on her lap.

"I'm here for you," he said. "I promise. I'll take you away—help you forget about everything. We'll change together—we'll escape these worlds."

"Why are you being like this?" Brandi asked. "I mean, I just walked into your apartment, all drugged up, threw up all over your floor, and you're still here listening to me."

"I guess that's love," Ravi said.

She lay down on the couch, her head on Ravi's lap. He lowered his head and kissed her, smelling beer and mucus. She kissed back and didn't let go. She turned around her chest against his. She pulled back.

"Do you mind if I crash here tonight?" Brandi asked. "I can sleep on the couch. I just need to be here tonight."

Ravi looked around the room, shoes tapping against the floor.

"Sure," he said. "But you can take the bed. I'll rest on the couch."

"Or we can both sleep in the bed. I really don't take up much space."

"No, I probably won't be able to sleep anyway. Take the bed. No problem at all."

She got up, pulling Ravi up, as well.

"Stay with me until I fall asleep," she said.

31

The telephone rang, and Ravi picked it up after the first ring.

"Hey Brandi," he said, without waiting to see who it was on the other line.

"Wow," she said. "You actually picked up the phone."

It had been a few days since Brandi had come over and slept at his place. They had had a wonderful time lying in bed while she told him more stories about her childhood and he tried to keep his to himself.

"I'm on my way to a friend's place," Brandi said. "He's having some people over."

Ravi didn't say anything.

"Would you want to come with me?" Brandi asked. "Keep me company?"

Ravi hesitated.

"Sure."

She told him to meet her at a coffee shop next to the guy's house. As soon as he hung up the phone and walked out the door, he became nervous. It had been a while since he had been to a college party—or any party for that matter. He was the guy who usually stood outside, chain-smoking, staring into the plants, and silently cursing the other people. Usually, about twenty minutes later, he would leave.

She was standing outside the café, wearing a black skirt with thin black stockings underneath. On top, she wore a button-up, red-collared shirt with the sleeves rolled up to the middle of her arm. Her hair was down, and Ravi could smell the fruit-scented shampoo from a few feet away. He was wearing jeans, a T-shirt, and the tattered pink coat he had washed several times to rid any traces of Vavi's blood from it. Though the coat was torn, it still gave Ravi comfort. It reminded him of happiness. He had no clue what his hair looked like—he hadn't touched it in days.

She lightly touched her hand against Ravi's face to feel the tenderness.

"Your face looks better," she said, "but you aren't looking so well."

"You want to get some coffee first before we go?"

They walked inside the café. The place was crowded and full of murmur and chatter. The espresso machines and blenders sporadically interrupted the people's discussions. They got their mochas and found seats in the corner of the café. Ravi asked Brandi how she was doing.

"Okay. I'm taking a couple of days off. I wanted to paint, but I just can't get myself to do it right now."

She told him that she was planning to stay in Seattle for the summer, and she wanted to do as much artwork as possible.

"But the thing is, will I do it?" she asked. "Come on, let's go."

Ravi didn't want to go. He wanted to sit at the café with Brandi and lose himself in the echoes of other people's voices.

As they approached the guy's house, he could hear a mixture of music and voices. He became nervous again and walked slower than Brandi. She turned around.

"Thanks for coming."

She grabbed his hand, and they entered the house where the faint noises of music and voices had become vibrantly louder. The people at the front of the house automatically looked at them, and Ravi looked at Brandi. She smiled, and they continued to walk. Some people were dancing while others had formed their separate groups, and they had spread themselves throughout the living room and the rest of the house. Brandi didn't flinch at all while Ravi looked at the floor as they walked. She was still holding his hand as they walked into the kitchen. The house was dark, lit only by black and red lights while a disco ball swirled in the living room.

"You want something to drink?" Brandi asked.

"I'm okay. Maybe later I'll get something. Stay away from the Valium, right?"

"Right," Brandi said.

She took a red plastic cup and made herself a beverage, mixing Vodka with sparkling water. A couple of guys came up to them.

"Still sticking with the pink coat," one of the guys said.

He was one of the guys from the coffee shop where Ravi had run into Brandi.

"Sure," Ravi said.

The guy had a big smile on his face, and Ravi thought that it wasn't the nice type of smile, but more of the teasing kind. The guys talked to Brandi, and Ravi pretended to listen as he looked around the rooms—pretty people intermingling, laughing, dancing, and shouting. Clusters of blues, greens, and yellows marked their heads, lit every couple of seconds with the slow-moving disco ball hanging from the ceiling. He looked at one of the guys standing next to Brandi.

"Where's the bathroom?" Ravi asked.

The guy pointed to a door down the hallway, and Ravi told him thanks and went outside to smoke a cigarette. A few people made their way to the house as Ravi sat on the steps, and they said hello to him. Ravi politely replied and watched them walk into the house. He looked through the window and saw a guy standing by himself in the far corner of the living room, a red plastic cup in his hand, and he was looking around the room. The guy wore jeans, a tucked-in bright blue shirt, and bright white shoes. The shirt looked too big for his body, and his jeans looked too tight. One hand was in his pocket, and he stood as one would stand in wintry weather. He looked like he had just had his hair cut, too.

Not too far away from him were Brandi and one of her friends. He had short brown hair, spiked up, and his forearms were huge. Brandi appeared to be looking around, and Ravi guessed that she was looking for him. He smoked half his cigarette and put it out in a flowerpot that had become an ashtray during the party. He walked in and went straight to Brandi. She smiled and put her arm around his. *It feels good to have our arms entangled*, Ravi thought. She always knew when to touch him and how to touch him.

"How's it going, Pink?" the guy asked.

Ravi didn't answer him and looked straight into his eyes. Both his ears were lined with earring hoops, one of them chained to his nose ring. Ravi wanted to yank it out. He looked at the lonely guy standing in the corner.

Another guy walked up. He was wearing camouflage pants and a tight brown shirt, exposing his lack of muscle. It was Zippo.

"I can't believe he came," he said. "He doesn't even really know anyone here. I don't even know how he knew about the party."

"Maybe he's trying to make friends," Ravi replied.

The two laughed.

"Good luck," Zippo said.

"Don't worry about him," Ravi replied. "Just go about your business, son."

They looked at Ravi with crooked eyebrows, and their cheeks sucked in. *Good*, Ravi thought. He wanted them to be mad at him. His social anxiety was gone, and though he didn't feel in place, he didn't feel out of place, either. He found himself somewhere in the middle, confident and at ease. Brandi smiled at Ravi and shook her head.

"Be nice," she said.

"Yeah," Nose Ring said. "Be nice. You weren't invited, either."

"Oh, I just thought I'd do you guys a favor and show up. Give the people something to look at."

The guys half scowled, half smiled. Brandi broke into laughter.

Both guys walked away, bumping Ravi as they passed. Zippo turned around.

"You got a problem?" he asked.

"*You* got a problem," Ravi replied.

They walked away. Brandi was still smiling, but it was more like a "what are you doing" smile rather than the delighted kind.

"Sorry," Ravi said. "Didn't mean to."

"It's okay, but really, be careful. Those guys aren't afraid to fight."

"No worries."

Ravi was worried about getting into a fight. He didn't know how to be a tough guy, but he thought that he was doing okay. He was outnumbered, too. *At least they walked away.*

"I'm a tough guy," Ravi said and laughed.

"That's my ex," Brandi said. "His name is Will. This is his house."

She pointed to Zippo.

"The other guy, with the nose ring, that's Darrin—they're really good friends."

"That's your ex?" Ravi replied. "How'd you end up with *that* guy?"

"I know. I know. I told you I liked the jerks."

Brandi mentioned to Ravi that she was going to the bathroom, and then she was going to find a couple of her friends whom she hadn't talked to in a long time.

"You going to be okay?" Brandi asked, "I don't want to come back and find you in a garbage bin."

"I'll be alright."

Ravi walked to the guy standing alone in the corner. He looked at Ravi, smiled as he nodded his head, and took a sip from his cup. Ravi, standing a few feet away from him, nodded his head in return and smiled. He leaned against the wall. They stood silently for about five minutes before Ravi started a conversation.

"How's it going?"

The guy had a big smile on his face.

"Hi, I'm Max," he said, taking another sip.

"Having a good time?" Ravi asked.

"Yeah. I like watching people having a fun time. It's nice to be around it."

"Nice. I'm kind of the same way."

"I haven't seen you around before."

"Yeah, I know. I'm just friends with someone here—Brandi."

"Oh yes. Brandi. She's really nice."

"Yeah. She's great."

"She's the only one that really talks to me."

"Yeah, she's a nice one," Ravi said, nodding his head.

"Look," the guy said. "I don't know what you heard about me, but whatever it is, it's not true."

"Like what?"

"Some of the guys seem to think that I urinate in my pants regularly. I just happen to spill a lot of drinks on my clothes."

Ravi couldn't help but laugh.

"That's funny," Ravi said. "I guess it puts you in an

awkward situation. Forget them."

Max nodded his head and continued to grin. Ravi thought it might even be the biggest smile he had ever given. He stuck out his hand.

"I'm Ravi."

Max told Ravi that he wanted to be an English teacher, but he may go for a Ph.D. before he went on to teaching. He liked to read, write, and watch movies—the usual. Like Vavi, Max enjoyed science fiction a lot, but he didn't want to write science fiction. He told Ravi some authors and books he liked—Ravi didn't recognize any of them, but thought that they sounded interesting. They continued to stand by the wall, not talking for a few minutes. Brandi was mingling with the crowd.

"I have these terrible daydreams," Ravi said. "For the past few years, I see myself hanging in a ghost town. And there's a cowboy hat below my feet. It's evening, and I'm slightly swaying."

Max took a sip.

"Sorry," Ravi said. "Don't mean to come off as crazy or anything."

"Not at all," Max said. "That's interesting, though. Must be scary or frustrating."

Ravi asked him if he wanted to go outside with him to keep him company while he smoked. Max didn't look too comfortable with the idea, as he stuttered and looked around the room, but he decided to go anyway. They sat on the steps, and Ravi lit a cigarette.

"You want one?" Ravi asked.

"No thanks," Max replied. "Not really a smoker. Or a drinker either. I'm just drinking some orange juice."

Ravi didn't know what else to talk about, so he told Max about his homeless brother.

"Wow," Max said. "That's not good. What do you plan

to do?"

"I'm not sure."

"Maybe you should get him some professional help, and while you're at it, get some for yourself, too."

He rocked back and forth and laughed.

"Yeah. I know. I've thought about it, but I'm not sure."

As they sat on the steps, and as Ravi smoked cigarette after cigarette, the guy who was once standing in the corner by himself—shy, nervous, and out of place—transformed into a new person. He talked with gestures, conversed, and listened, and his tone of voice had much more strength to it. As he grew, Ravi realized that he, himself, was growing, too. Maybe they wouldn't have a long-lasting friendship, maybe he wouldn't see him ever again, but for now—for right now—Ravi was communicating. *Thanks, Brandi.*

"So how come you don't talk to anyone at the party?" Ravi asked.

"We don't really have anything in common, I guess," Max said. "I just like to come and observe the people. It's nice to be around people who are having fun. And I don't think anyone really likes me, anyway."

"So, you don't really have any friends?" Ravi asked.

"No. Not really. My boyfriend and I just broke up. I guess I'm just finally getting out of it—trying to be more social again. I took it pretty bad."

"I'm sorry about that. I hope you find whatever you're looking for, though. And same here—I guess Brandi is really the only friend I have."

"Thanks. Yeah, it gets tough sometimes," Max said. "Feeling lonely and all.

"It's weird how you get used to it—so used to it that you feel even lonelier when you're around people, you know? Feeling awkward when you're around people, you know?"

"Exactly," Max said. "And you keep on thinking that

things will change. That you'll meet someone or that you'll get friends and all that."

Ravi nodded his head and exhaled smoke.

"So, what brought you all together?" Max asked.

"Spilt beer and kindness, I guess. It's weird. She's almost the exact opposite of me. She likes to talk and open up, and I, on the other hand, tend to keep to myself. But I love it. I like what we have. It's more interesting this way. It's all new to me."

Ravi went on and on about Brandi. He felt bad—he had opened up to Max about his feelings more than he had to Brandi. She deserved to hear this. She deserved to know that he was in love with her, that he loved her. He realized now why she was frustrated with him. She wanted to hear the words that he was now saying to Max. She knew he was thinking it, but she wanted to hear it, and Ravi had never said anything. It seemed like it had been going too fast, but with all the slowness in his life, Ravi finally realized that the fast felt nice. It was a good change of pace for him.

Ravi and Max continued to talk about friendships and relationships. Ravi smoked about five cigarettes by now, but he didn't remember lighting any of them except for the first one. He could tell that Max didn't get the chance to talk about himself too often. He seemed like he had a lot on his mind. He had a lot to say.

They both arrived at the point where they didn't know what they were talking about, but they continued to converse anyway—Ravi liked being around Max. They exchanged phone numbers, and Max asked Ravi if he would like to go watch a movie or get something to eat with him sometime. The door opened behind them, and Brandi came out. Ravi wanted to tell her that he loved her.

"There you are," she said. "I thought you had left."

"Sorry."

"Hey, Max," Brandi said.

He waved his hand.

"What are you guys doing?" Brandi asked. "Staying out of trouble?"

"Nothing much," Ravi said. "Just talking. You know, communicating with people."

He smiled. Brandi asked Ravi if he wanted to leave in about ten or fifteen minutes, and he told her yes. They all went back inside. Max walked to the same corner of the living room, and Ravi went to the kitchen where Brandi was talking to a small group of friends, including her ex-boyfriend.

"Hello there," a lady said.

Ravi didn't reply. He looked at a couple of the guys—they were looking at his shoes.

"Nice coat," she said.

Will walked up to Ravi and stood right beside him and leaned his face in. His breath smelled of beer, and his eyes, Ravi could tell, were past drunkenness.

"So, what exactly do you do?" Will asked. Why are you here? How do you know Brandi?"

"All good questions," Ravi said, looking at Brandi. "You ready to go?"

Brandi nodded her head, put her arm around Ravi's, and told the other people bye. As they left the kitchen, Ravi felt a hand on the back of his shoulder. It was a strong grasp, pinching his skin through his clothes, making him groan. Ravi turned around as he pushed the hand aside. Will stood before him—his eyes were dark red, and he was sweating and breathing loudly. Before Ravi could say or do anything, Will hit him in the stomach, causing him to fall to his knees.

"Fuck."

Ravi got back up and tackled him to the floor. This was a challenging task to do, as he was much bigger than Ravi, but Will's drunkenness helped Ravi knock him to the tiles. Ravi got on top of him, straddling him, pinning his arms against the floor, and Will spat in his face. Ravi spat back, and then slapped him in the face—a hard slap, leaving a red mark on his cheek. Will managed to push Ravi off with his knees and kicked Ravi while they both were on the ground. They both got up as quickly as possible. Ravi was still a little winded from the punch. Will was a little winded from the alcohol. A crowd surrounded them—some shouting to stop, others shouting in support of Will. Ravi could hear Brandi's voice telling both to stop. Will tried to land a punch, but he was short of hitting Ravi's face, leaving him in an open position. Ravi punched him in the nose, causing his eyes to water. He let out a whimper and covered his face. But as Ravi tried to punch him one more time in the stomach, Will gave two quick jabs to Ravi's face. Ravi didn't feel anything. He moved back, throwing two punches himself, both missing Will's cheek. Then they got into a punching frenzy. Circling each other with one eye closed and hoping their knuckles would feel something. They both got some hits in, but Ravi was the first to fall, facing the ground. He felt a rope wrapped around his neck, moving in a circular motion like a boa constrictor around its prey, causing such friction that it felt like his body was on fire. Ravi could feel his teeth grinding against each other, and he managed to stand up with his fists closed, ready for another punching fit. *He has me*, Ravi thought. Will walked toward Ravi, but he didn't do anything, and then he slowly moved back as he stared at him. Ravi walked up to him with his hands raised, fists opened.

"Come here," Ravi said. "Wait."

He stopped moving away. Ravi went up to him and whispered in his ear.

"Let's stop this. Stop it. Leave Brandi alone. It's time to

grow up."

Ravi looked him in the eyes. Will struggled to look back.

"It's done. It'll be okay. It's done."

He felt a tug on his arm—a gentle tug. Brandi put her arm around Ravi's and guided him out of the kitchen and through the living room. Before they left the house, they went to the corner of the living room where Max was standing. This time he was talking to someone. He smiled and waved to Ravi and Brandi. Max's friend turned around and looked at them. He looked timid—just as shy as Max had looked when Brandi and Ravi had arrived at the party. They waved back and left the house.

Ravi had been in quite a few fights before, and these excluded all the ones he had had with his brother. All of them were in high school. It was amazing how people wanted to pick on those who just wanted to be alone. He didn't like fighting in high school, but he felt like he had to do it to defend himself. Other than with Vavi, he hadn't fought anyone until the party that day. There was a sense of guilt that would always overcome him after a fight, but this time, he felt fine. There was no guilt at all. He felt refreshed.

"You have a new friend now," Brandi said as they walked outside—as if nothing had happened in the kitchen.

"Yeah. I guess so. I like Max. He's a nice guy."

"Oh, I know," Brandi said. "We should all go out to eat one day."

Brandi grabbed his arm, and she stopped walking, causing Ravi to stop. She looked into his eyes and moved her lips close to his ears.

"You are a fighter," she whispered.

Ravi shook his head.

"Not at all," he whispered back. "I didn't know what I really was doing. I'm sorry you had to see that. I should have walked away. I don't like to fight, but I didn't know what else to do."

Brandi combed his hair with her fingers.

"Yeah," she said. "You should have, but I understand. I'm done with all of that. Guys and fighting and ex-boyfriends. Feels like you'll be looking like a raccoon for quite some time now."

It was around midnight as Brandi and Ravi left the house. She wanted to go back to the coffee house. The place would be open for another hour, so they decided to get some mochas.

"You had a fun time?" Ravi asked.

"Yeah. It was okay. Did you?"

"Yeah. Thanks for asking me to come."

"See," Brandi said. "It wasn't so bad after all. Except for the fight. And you met Max. Better than sitting alone at a bar and drinking by yourself."

"Yeah, but that's how we met."

"What did you whisper in Will's ear?"

"Nothing much," Ravi said. "I just told him to grow up, and that it's done."

She raised her eyebrows and twirled her hair. Ravi ran his hand through his hair and started to twirl it, as well. He saw her smile, which she seemed to be trying to hide. It was then that Ravi realized how comfortable he felt being around Brandi. The knee shaking, the fidgeting and not looking at her, and the fiddling with his hands were all gone. They talked. They talked like they had been friends for a million years. They talked like they were in a relationship.

"Will you go out with me again?" Brandi asked, smirking.

It was like she knew what Ravi was thinking about—him and her.

"Only if you buy me some roses."

They looked around the coffee shop, noticing that there were barely any people inside, and it didn't look like the same café they had gone to only a few hours earlier. Ravi lit a cigarette.

"I guess I never really told you," he said, "but I'm glad it was you and no one else."

"What do you mean?"

"I mean I'm glad it was you who found me. No matter what happens, I'm glad it was you."

As she laughed, Ravi was taken away from the café. His body was still there. He was still sitting with Brandi, and the sound of blenders and beeps was still present, but amidst all this, Ravi saw himself hanging in those familiar surroundings. The cowboy hat was still there, and a light-brown rope wrapped around his neck. The evening, as always, was beautiful as the sun made its way below the horizon. This vision flickered in and out, first with Brandi's face, and then Vavi's. Then Vavi came back into his mind.

"Ravi," Brandi said.

Ravi was back at the café, both physically and mentally. She had been calling his name several times.

"Sorry," Ravi said. "Kind of lost me for a minute there."

"Are you okay?"

"I have dreams of myself hanging," Ravi said like it was an everyday occurrence. "I think I hang myself. And it's like in one of those cowboy settings, and there's no one else around. Just me. And I think I'm dead. I've been having these dreams for years. And I'm getting tired of it. No matter how hard I've tried, I can't get rid of it. It haunts me day to day. I think of you—I think of Vavi and my parents, but at the end, I'm dead with a noose around my neck."

"Strange," Brandi said. "I've had reoccurring dreams before, but never for that long, and never that horrible."

"It's kind of annoying."

Brandi put her hand on top of his and rubbed his knuckles.

"I wish you would have told me earlier about this," she said. "No wonder you keep to yourself. That must be horrible."

"I got used to it, but lately it's taking its toll. I'm ready to move on."

"Just give it some time. Come to me. Stop keeping to yourself—you need people around you."

Her care for me is amazing, Ravi thought. He had never met someone who cared so much for others. He had been estranged from this feeling for so long.

They left the café and walked back to her place. She put *Jurassic Park* into the DVD player, and they sat on the couch, her head against his shoulder, his head against her head. Ravi's eyes felt heavy, and they eventually closed, until he heard Brandi whisper in his ear.

"I want to make you forget about those dreams. Dream about me."

Ravi looked at her—the tip of her nose tickled his. Her eyes were large and round, glassy, filled with welcoming amour. Her hands were on his lap. She kissed his eyebrows, his cheeks, and his nose. She got off the couch and took off her skirt and then her shoes. She sat down next to Ravi and tilted her head toward him, and he tilted his head toward her. Their lips met somewhere in the middle, and Ravi found himself in a circus—loud music, hundreds of people shouting and laughing, elephants and tigers dancing, and there was the smell of freshly made popcorn and roasted peanuts roaming the air.

He didn't know how long they kissed, and to him, it seemed like time, space, all matter tangible and intangible, vanished or had been sucked into their mouths and distributed throughout their bodies by their circulatory systems. She took her shirt off and placed it on the carpet like it was breakable. She did the same with Ravi's shirt. She placed each of her hands on the sides of his face and kissed him again, and Ravi, again, became lost. She took his hands and guided them around her body. Ravi closed his eyes and followed her. He closed his eyes, and his hands traced her body from belly button to chest, lips, and eyes. He closed his eyes and hid his face in her chest, trying to escape from the world, but the world followed him as he saw snapshots of himself hanging, dead, eyes opened, hands limped against his side. The wind was strong this time, and he shook back and forth as the wooden platform creaked and sang to the dimming sun. He closed his eyes harder as she unbuttoned his pants.

32

Ravi woke up the next morning on the couch. Brandi was already gone, but she left a note in his shoe saying that she was going to eat breakfast with her parents and that she would call him later. At the end of the note, she drew a smiley face.

Ravi's vision was strange. He saw everything in a light like everything had a spotlight shining on it. He felt light like there was no gravity. He took a shower and put on some fresh clothes that Brandi had left for him on the kitchen table. He breathed. He smiled. He was still in a daze. He didn't know where he was; he knew where he was, and he wanted to cry, but nothing came out.

Ravi used to watch his mother dress as she was getting ready to go to Indian parties. He would sit on the bed as she stood in front of the mirror trying on different earrings, necklaces, and bracelets. The room was always kept dark when she was dressing, lit with a few candles and the lamp next to her bed. Ravi would ask her if he could try on some of her jewelry, and he would stand beside her while she slipped a sparkling bracelet around his wrist and the matching necklace around his neck. "When I'm gone," she would say, "you and Vavi will get all of these, and you can give them to your spouses." After they were gone, Ravi kept them in a box in his aunt's house. He especially liked watching his mother putting on the saris. It looked like some kind of ritual as she wrapped the cloth around her body, making carefully thought-out folds. The green and yellow sari was always his favorite. She would sing Tagore songs, while his father would be in the shower singing songs his mother used to sing to him when he was a child.

Ravi thought about his mother's saris as he walked back to the apartment where he saw Vavi standing outside. He was in the middle of taking off all his clothes. He stripped down until he only had on his underwear. His legs were thin, but they had tightly packed calf muscles. His body frame looked frail, like a duckling that had just been born. Ribs stuck out. His chest hair was almost in a perfect triangular shape. Around his neck was a gold chain—the one Ravi had given him for his twenty-seventh birthday. Vavi had forgotten that it was his birthday when Ravi visited him outside the café that day to give him his gift. Ravi thought that he had sold it since then because he had never seen him wear it until that day. Vavi had this smile on his face like he had a joke he had been dying to tell his brother.

"What are you doing?" Ravi asked frantically.

"Finished," Vavi said. "I'm finished with the manuscript."

His voice sounded like Father's when he used to talk to Mother about serious matters. From his bag, he took out a large stack of papers. And then he picked up his pants from the sidewalk and took out a crumpled piece of paper. He handed both to Ravi. On the crumpled piece of paper was a drawing of a giant futuristic jellyfish. It looked half robotic, and its tentacles were armed with small laser guns and sharp blades. It was in pencil, drawn lightly, like the tip of the granite had barely touched the paper. He was a great drawer. When they lived at home, Ravi would always ask his brother to draw him tigers, bears, and dinosaurs, and Ravi would hang them up on his wall. They were in a box now, kept in the closet. At the bottom of the jellyfish drawing, there was an inscription reading: "To my little brother. I love you so much."

"Well, you see," Vavi said. "There's this huge jellyfish

with these huge tentacles. It comes from the future through some time portal on accident, and the portal leads to an opening at the bottom of the Pacific Ocean. Despite its humungous size, the jellyfish is just a child, and so it's scared and angry all at the same time."

"Thanks," Ravi said. "I'll keep it with the others."

Ravi looked at the large stack of papers—it was his manuscript. The title page had *Tentacles Numbing* written on it. Ravi told Vavi that he was going to start reading it that night.

"And so, like, each tentacle takes over a continent," Vavi continued. "It sweeps over lands and knocks over buildings, kills people, total destruction, you know?"

Vavi swayed back and forth in his underwear in excitement. He loved the idea. Ravi pictured Vavi sitting behind the camera and directing where and how the jellyfish would attack, and how the people would run away in delirium.

"What about your clothes?" Ravi asked.

"I'm covered with delight—just give me a second. What about you? What happened to you? You look different. You look strong. Vibrant. Fresh."

Vavi grabbed his bag and took out a suit and a pair of polished black shoes. The suit was navy blue. He started putting it on.

"Do you want to go inside and put it on?"

"Of course not," Vavi replied.

He had this energy in him that Ravi hadn't seen in years. He finished dressing.

"We should celebrate the finished script," Vavi said. "Maybe you can take me out to eat one day. Your treat. Start reading the script, too."

He shook Ravi's hand and kissed him on the cheek.

"I look forward to seeing you," Vavi said, patting him

on the back.

"You, too."

Ravi had no clue what to think. Was this a new Vavi? A reinvigorated Vavi—the one who used to walk around the house whistling and joking around with everyone years ago at the house? He couldn't remember the last time he saw his brother completely sober. Ravi took the script up to his apartment and sat on the bed, staring at the closet—its door was open, and he saw a cardboard box with the flaps opened. He walked over and took out his mother's green and yellow sari.

It happened all in one motion—without thinking, he stripped down and started wrapping the garment around his body. He had seen his mother do it enough times to where he didn't have to wonder how to wear the sari. Ravi draped the cloth around his waist, tucked one end tightly, and covered his shoulder with the other end. Looking in the mirror, he didn't see his mother—he saw ribs, growing bruises, and a bloated stomach looking much like a balloon. His chest hair was barely hanging on to his skin. He walked to the toilet bowl, throwing up and dry gagging. It was mainly phlegm mixed with some blood. He kept the sari on as he lay in bed, hoping the scent of its fading perfume would lull him to sleep.

33

While his aunt was sleeping, Ravi took her Mercedes out for a ride. He drove by Brandi's place in the middle of the night, around one in the morning. When she opened the door, he didn't want to blink—he didn't want to miss any second of seeing her in her light blue pajama pants and white undershirt, face smoothed from the lotion he could smell.

"What's wrong?" she asked.

"Come on. Hurry."

"Where?"

"Just come on."

"Wait, let me get my shoes."

"No time for that, but bring a phonebook."

He grabbed her arm and led her to the car. As he drove, she kept on asking him where they were going. Ravi avoided answering and sang a horrible version of Salt-N-Pepa's "Shoop." They reached their destination—the automated car wash.

"Are you serious?" Brandi asked.

She half laughed, half mumbled.

"It's too late for a carwash."

"It's never too late for a rainbow."

They entered the tunnel, waiting for the red light to turn on, letting him know when to stop and turn the car off. The water started spraying on all sides of the car. Then the huge, spinning blue foam brushes swiped the sides of the car.

"Couldn't you have waited until the morning to do this?"

He told her to look and pointed at the front windshield.

Splashes of green, purple, blue, yellow, orange, and red pounded the car. Rainbow soap. They sat silently, admiring the view. All that they could hear was the soap and water hitting the car and the twirling of the foam brushes. It was a muffled sound, like when Ravi would hide his head in his pillow, covering his ears, but the world still existed outside in a quiet song coming from miles away in the wind.

"Welcome to my carnival," Ravi said.

Brandi placed her hand on his shoulder as the colorful drops were sprayed off with the rinsing cycle. Then a new set of dark yellow foam brushes appeared to dry the car.

"Look," Ravi said. "I may not be good with words—with opening up and all that. We both know this. But I just wanted to let you know what I see when I see you. I see those colorful raindrops passing through my eyes. That's what I think of you."

Brandi didn't say anything. The carwash finished and he pulled out and went toward the interstate.

"Where are we going now?" Brandi asked.

Her voice, soft and quivering, let him know that she was touched—it let him know that he had gotten his message across. He didn't answer and started singing again—not a particular song, but just random words mixed with the lyrics of various songs. His mouth finally dried up just as they pulled into a parking lot looking over the beach.

"Come on," Ravi said.

He ran around to the other side of the car and helped her out. With his arm around her, they ran through a gate he had broken years ago, back when he would go there regularly to think about his parents.

As they walked in darkness to find a place to sit, he could only tell that the beach was there by the smell of the salt, the sound of the tides sliding in, and the faint reflections of the moon on the water. They planted their bodies in the sand and felt the gritty cold texture of the grains clinging to their feet and arms. Brandi leaned her head against his shoulder as they looked at the waves.

"This is too nice," she said.

"Thought maybe we could take a quick getaway from the rest of the world for a bit."

"You know, I feel sweet when I'm around you. All that fuck-this-fuck-that-art-and-philosophy stuff, it all goes away, and I feel somewhat disgusted when I think about it like I'm losing who I am."

"I don't think you should throw it all away," Ravi said. "You really do have a passion for art. I can see it when you talk about it."

"Thanks," Brandi said. "It all makes sense when I'm around you."

She grabbed a handful of sand and poured it down his pants and laughed.

Ravi tried to do the same to her, and he wanted to tell her that he felt the same way—that he lost himself a long time ago; that he had quit trying to see who he was after the death of his parents and after Vavi had left for the streets. But he didn't mention it—at that moment, he didn't want anything to get in the way. He was happy.

After the beach, they didn't go home.

"Did you bring the phonebook?" Ravi asked.

"Yeah, why?"

"Look up where Max lives."

"You're kidding me."

"Tonight's the night we all have a night."

Ravi remembered the last time he had felt this goofy—when everyone was still alive and together and they were all at the Playhouse eating pizza and playing Skee-ball, arcade games like those car racing ones where one would have to sit down and press down on a pedal and shift the gears with the right hand and use the steering wheel with the left. It was the last time he could remember feeling carefree, unrestricted from all thought, just going with the feeling of excitement and joy. This was just before he went into high school, a year before his parents were killed. Everyone was smiling—his father, mother, and brother. Ravi wished he could put all his memories in a box and throw it in the ocean.

It took Max a long time to answer the door. After a couple of knocks, they rang the doorbell a few times. A few minutes later, Brandi and Ravi saw a light come on through the window, and Max peered through the blinds. He opened the door and asked if everything was okay. The right side of his face was red from sleeping hard on it. He was wearing a baggy T-shirt bearing the face of Martin Luther King and a pair of plaid boxers.

"You weren't sleeping, were you?" Ravi asked.

"It's, like, almost three in the morning?"

"Well come on then," Ravi said. "We've got to get going."

Brandi grabbed Max's arm and pulled him out the door. He didn't speak in the car, and Ravi blared the radio to keep him from sleeping. They pulled into the parking lot of a 24-hour restaurant—Delly's. It was one of those Fifties-themed restaurants, and there was a jukebox. There was no one inside except for a couple of waiters and a cook. Despite the lack of people, the place was comfortable and welcoming with the bright lights and Dion's song about a lady named Sue.

They all ordered chocolate malts. Max had finally woken up, and they sat and talked about nonsense. Brandi laughed and called them geeks as they goofed around and talked about Star Wars. It was a great laugh—one that came from the feet and moved all the way up to the brain and then back down through the mouth. It was pure. Max went on to talk about the novel he was writing. It was a horror about vicious kangaroos in Australia.

"It's like *Pet Cemetery*," Max said. "But with kangaroos."

Brandi talked about art—Picasso, Van Gogh, Gauguin, and a couple of names Ravi had never heard before like Klimt and De Chirico. He printed those names on a napkin, and underneath the table, she playfully rubbed his thigh. He looked at her, her face painted with amusement, all scrunched up, a little ball of energy. Ravi thought she must have felt as he had felt when he was at the Playhouse with his family. He barely spoke for the rest of the night but listened to Brandi and Max talk about their passions— reading, writing, art, philosophy, movies, and relationships. Max was still talking about the guy whom he had met at the party.

"Who knows—let's see how it goes," Max said.

Brandi put her hand on top of Ravi's and said she didn't want the night to end. She had this glow to her—the same glow he saw in those pictures at her parents' house. Ritchie Valens was playing in the background. Max took the last whirling sip of his chocolate shake, and Ravi thought about hanging himself.

34

As Ravi walked through the aisles of Barnes and Noble, he tried to remember the last time he had visited the bookstore—it had been so long, he couldn't recall. He used to go all the time, either with Vavi or by himself. Whenever he would go with Vavi to the bookstore, they would make sentences out of the titles on the shelves. Some could be quite creative, while others made no sense at all. Vavi took time with his, though, carefully constructing poems out of his titles, while Ravi's were mainly incomprehensible. It had gotten to the point where he had known all the employees by name, and they knew his.

When he went this time, he didn't recognize any of the faces except for one of the managers. As they walked by each other, she looked like she wanted to say hi, but she gave a faint smile instead. He just walked through the mazes, gazing at the titles, running his fingers across their spines.

He walked to the film section and imagined Vavi's screenplay on the shelf next to Spike Lee's. From there he went to the children's section and looked at the Hardy Boys series. These were the first books that made him want to read more. Vavi had given all of his collection to him, and he'd torn through them, three books per week during the summertime. What happened to those days?

After the bookstore, Ravi checked to see if Vavi was sitting outside the coffee shop. He was there, dressed in his suit, crouching down, smoking a cigarette, and staring at the sidewalk. Ravi tapped him on the shoulder. Without looking at him, Vavi said, "Come on, let's go back to the park." He wasn't drunk. He stood up, and Ravi followed behind him, noticing the creases in the back of his pants and the dirt smudged on his jacket. His neck looked so frail that Ravi wanted to place his hand on it to keep it warm— to keep it from breaking.

They walked past the bench where they had fought to the corner of the park where Ravi saw a mound of dirt neatly patted. Vavi turned around and looked at him for the first time, noticing his new bruises. He ran his hand down one side of Ravi's face.

"Not sure how long the city is going to let me keep it, but I'm going to try for as long as they let me," Vavi said.

"What is it?"

"I'm growing a garden here."

Ravi stared at the dirt, not saying anything.

"For you and me," Vavi said.

He stared at the mound, as well, lighting a cigarette and brushing off his pants.

"This is the new beginning," he continued. "For you and me."

Vavi sat down on the grass, and Ravi sat beside him, looking at him like he was about to read him a bedtime story.

"I've been lying," Vavi said. "I know you know. I'm not living as I should be. I've fallen, and I've lost my way, but now I'm seeing everything again."

Ravi opened his mouth to speak, but Vavi raised his hand, signaling that he was not finished talking yet.

"This is tough," Vavi said.

He looked up at the sky and squinted at the sun.

"I kind of touched on it before. I fucked up. I fucked up a lot. I shouldn't have left you. I shouldn't have left. You needed me, I know, and I needed you, but I ran away from it all."

"It's okay, though," Ravi said.

"Well, we're lucky," Vavi said. "We're lucky we're still alive. Look at you, man. You look like you're on your deathbed. And I know I'm at least part of the reason for this. I'm sorry."

Ravi lit a cigarette and grazed his hand over the grass.

"I can't tell you how many times I've thought about killing myself," Vavi said. "Just giving up and getting away from it all. But you—I always thought about you, and that's why I'm still here."

"Same here," Ravi said.

"It has been through quite a struggle, you and me. We need a change. It's going to hurt—it's going to take a while, but I just wanted to let you know that I'm going to be okay. Honestly. I'm going to be okay. I'm leaving the streets. I'm going back to Auntie's house for good—to regroup, regain my strength."

Ravi's knees shook in excitement, like a dog's tail. He wanted to shout and run around the park. He felt like he was sitting beside the quiet, enlightened Vavi again—the one who opened up to the world for him, through his own silent kind of way. The one who stood in the corner of the basketball court, waiting for the ball to be passed to him so that he could shoot the winning shot.

"You should come with me, too. It'll be better for both of us."

Living with Vavi again. His thoughts were everywhere—full of energy and hope. Ravi nodded his head. They both stood up and faced each other.

"And we'll work on this garden together as long as they let us."

"Sounds great," Ravi said.

"We still need to get dinner," Vavi said. "I'm going back to Auntie's this week. Make sure to check your answering machine and start packing. No rush, but you might just want to start now."

He stuck out his hand, and Ravi shook it. He patted Ravi on the back and said, "I'll see you soon," as he walked away.

35

At the cemetery, Brandi and Ravi were sitting on a small stone bench in front of Bruce Lee's grave. Max was there, as well, but had wandered off looking for the perfect name.

"I like to come here and think and relax," Ravi said. "It's quiet, you know, and I guess it's me opening up to the world in my own kind of way."

"Just you and Bruce," Brandi said.

"Just you, me, and Bruce. So. You wanted to know some more about me, here is something. I like to visit Bruce Lee's grave. It's like your corner in the library."

She didn't say anything.

"I want to buy you chocolate."

"I know," Brandi replied.

They sat quietly and let everything either soak in or flood out—Ravi wasn't sure which one was happening. He just wanted to sit there for a few more minutes and enjoy his company in silence. Brandi wanted to do this, as well. They talked to each other through their breathing and blinking, letting the sun cozily warm the back of their necks.

Ravi told Brandi that he had to go to the apartment and get ready for dinner with Vavi.

"When am I going to meet him?" Brandi asked.

He told her soon, but not just yet. He told her that Vavi was changing—that it looked like he was not going to be homeless anymore, but he didn't want to force anything, and he wanted to see what Vavi would say that night.

"How are your dreams going?" Brandi asked.

"I just had one, actually."

Brandi pouted her lips. Ravi lied and told her that it

wasn't about him hanging.

"But it was about you," he said. "You were standing under the sun, shining—your smile could be seen from miles away."

He wished that was true.

She kissed him on the cheek. It was one of those small kisses—those pecks on the cheek and forehead that made him feel like he wanted to shake everyone's hands and tell them hello.

36

Vavi was standing outside the coffee shop where Ravi usually found him. He looked sharp in his navy blue suit. His hair was combed and parted to the side. His face was shaven, and Ravi could smell musky cologne as he approached his older brother. Ravi barely recognized him. He looked like Father. He stood there with a smile. Next to his feet was a brand-new laundry bag, bright and red. Next to the laundry bag was a briefcase.

They had dinner at a sandwich and soup restaurant. They both ordered bowls of chicken noodle soup with turkey and cheese sandwiches on toasted French bread.

"I got a job," Vavi said. "It turns out that living outside the coffee shop and not causing too much trouble gave me good credit. I asked the manager if I could pick up some shifts and, without hesitation, the manager said I can start training next week."

Ravi smiled so hard it hurt. He congratulated him. The good news didn't end there as Vavi and Ravi talked about the future. Vavi was going to start submitting his manuscript to companies and agencies while he worked at the café. He already liked someone who worked at the café, and he wanted to see if he could go out with her. Ravi listened and listened. He listened to his voice, strong and confident. Determined. He saw his eyes. They didn't waver, but looked directly into his, giving off an energy of love. Ravi soaked it in as he nodded his head to everything he said.

"I read your script," Ravi said. "And loved it. Really loved it."

"That's great—thanks. But let's not talk about that

now."

Though Ravi wasn't hungry, he forced himself to eat the soup and sandwich. He must because Vavi wanted to treat him to dinner.

"When are you going to move in?" Vavi asked.

"Soon enough. I'm almost done packing. Maybe in a couple of days."

"Great."

After dinner, they walked back to the coffee shop. They didn't say much. They both had so much going on in their minds. Ravi's excitement and energy had worn him out. He hugged his brother—a strong hug—and he didn't let go for ten seconds. He kissed Vavi on the forehead and told him to kiss each side of his face. Vavi did what Ravi asked.

Their grandfather, on Father's side, asked them to do that when they had visited him in Kolkata. Each night he would sit in a broken chair in his living room, staring into space, and he would call them from the room they were staying in to hug him before he went to bed. Ravi remembered the last time he wished him goodnight because it was the last time he saw him—his grandfather had passed away a few months later. The family had been visiting Kolkata for the summer. It had been Ravi's first trip to India that he was old enough to remember. It was their last night in Kolkata before they had to travel back to Seattle, and his grandfather, Dada, was sitting in the living room after dinner, as always. He sat and stared at nothing as if nothing was a world to him. When he had called Vavi and Ravi into the living room to wish them goodnight, he stood up this time. He hugged both of them, and then he asked them to kiss him on his forehead and each cheek. He hugged them again. It was this last hug that gave Ravi a chill. He looked deeply into Ravi's eyes and managed a smile as he rubbed his knuckles against Ravi's cheek. He told him he loved him. He told him to look after his brother, and he said the same to Vavi. Ravi didn't realize until years later that Dada knew that he wasn't going to see them again.

Vavi patted Ravi on the back and opened the door to the coffee shop.

"See you in a couple days," Ravi shouted.

"Yes. See you, brother."

37

At the apartment, he called Brandi for the first time—she didn't pick up the phone, so he left her a voicemail: "Brandi. Hi Brandi. Hey, I love you. I love you, I love you, I love you. Take care."

He put on the pink coat. *So this is happiness*, he thought. This was what it felt like. Like loving the entire world. Like loving everything around you. Everything was in a lighter tint. Nothing mattered. Pure joy. Smiling. Crying. Laughing from the lungs. Goosebumps on the arms. Wanting to be. Wanting to exist. Wanting to be around. Feeling important.

As he unwrapped the rope around his lamp, he thought about Vavi and Brandi. He thought about Vavi's future. He saw his brother's name appearing in the opening credits of the movie: "Screenplay written by Vavi Bosh." He saw him in his navy blue suit, serving coffee to customers, never letting go of his smile.

With the rope resting on his shoulder, he took the chair from the kitchen and walked to the basement of the apartment complex. Images of Brandi flickered. Her smile. Her hair was tied in a ponytail. Kissing. On the couch—her skin, tan and comforting. Coffee shop, sitting across from each other, laughing and talking. Her hand upon his. At the bar, her pink coat. Her whispers.

In the basement, he placed the chair down right under a large black pipe set close to the ceiling that ran from wall to wall, and then he lit a cigarette. Standing on the chair, he wrapped the rope around the pipe and tied a noose. He loved his mother and father so much. Vavi. Brandi. He saw himself sitting on his mother's lap in the living room as she told his father to go get Vavi from upstairs so that they could go out for dinner. He smelled her lemon-scented skin. Father—shaking his hand, patting him on the back, kissing him on the cheek after he told him about his report card. His eyes gleamed. Mother's eyes glittered. Vavi is on the basketball court. Vavi sat across from him as they ate dinner. The greatest news. Brandi told him that she wanted him to forget about his dreams—telling him that she wanted him to dream about her.

"I love you all."

The tears blended in with the mucus right under his nose. This overwhelming sense of guilt. This overwhelming sense of happiness. *So this is happiness*, he thought again. This was delight in its purest form. Not a care.

He closed his eyes. He saw himself hanging. It wasn't haunting, though, but pleasant. Hanging, as usual, the sun descending, and the cowboy hat unmoved, but this time he wasn't alone. Vavi was there, smiling, holding his manuscript in hand. Brandi was there, too. She was laughing so hard that tears were coming down her cheeks. It was all muted, though. It was lovely. It was the best image he had ever seen. It was what he saw right before he set the rope and the chair on fire. It was a simple and quiet burn, going from the rope to the wooden chair—a gentle crackling, flooding his blood with warmth. He sat cross-legged on the floor and stared at the burning. The smoke rose to the top in a swirling motion, reminding him of his brother's black and cloudy marble. It set off the ceiling sprinklers. The dots of water tickled his skin. The collar of his pink coat, soaked and heavy and dirty, cooled the back of his neck. He sat and stared.

"Lovely," he whispered.

That was all he could say—lovely—and he sat there in the basement full of rain and looked past the fiery rope and chair, through the walls, and through the trees and traffic lights and cemeteries, and if he looked hard enough into the horizon, where the sun was cut in half, he could see a triceratops walking in the distance.

Acknowledgments

Tentacles Numbing couldn't have been created without the support, love, and care of the following lovely beings:

Thank you to my friends, who without hesitation, have always shown so much kindness and support—your friendship means so much, truly and sincerely.

Thank you, Mike Bourgeois and Andy LeGoullon. Thank you, Chad and Bianca Cosby. Thank you, Karl Schott and Mandy Migues. Thank You, Rien Fertel. Thank you, Andy Breaux. Thank you, Stacey and Terry Grow. Thank you, Luke Sonnier. Thank you, Patrick O'Neil. Thank You, Jennifer Ames. Thank you, Jerome Moroux. Thank you, Katie Culbert. Thank you, Story Frantzen, Abby Langford, and Jacob Camden. Thank you, Antioch University-Los Angeles, including Tara Ison, Susan Taylor Chehak, Dana Johnson, Dodie Bellamy, Leonard Chang, Tananarive Due, and Rob Roberge. Thank you, Chanel Martins, for your editorial guidance. Thank you, Chaya Bhuvaneswar, Elise Blackwell, and Anuja Varghese for your thoughtful and kind words. Thank you, Lafayette Barnes & Noble.

Many thanks to the Literary Community who has provided so much encouragement.

Thank you, Thirty West Publishing House—for all of this.

And to my parents, Sarmistha and Subrata Dasgupta, my brother, Deep, and my sister-in-law, Heidi—I love you all so much. Thank you, always, for being there. Love.

About the Author

Shome Dasgupta is the author of eleven books, including The *Seagull And The Urn* (HarperCollins India), *Cirrus Stratus* (Spuyten Duyvil), *Spectacles* (Word West Press), *i am here And You Are Gone* (Winner of the 2010 OW Press Fiction Contest), *Anklet And Other Stories* (Golden Antelope Press), & a poetry collection, *Iron Oxide* (Assure Press). His novel, *The Muu-Antiques*, is forthcoming from Malarkey Books. A hybrid collection of prose titled, *Histories Of Memories*, is forthcoming from Belle Point Press. His writing has appeared in *McSweeney's Internet Tendency*, *Hobart*, *New Orleans Review*, *X-R-A-Y*, *Arkansas Review*, *American Book Review*, *New Delta Review*, *Magma Poetry*, & elsewhere. His fiction & poetry have been anthologized in *Best Small Fictions 2019* & *Best Small Fictions 2021*, *The &Now Awards 2: The Best Innovative Writing*, & *Poetic Voices Without Borders 2*. His work has been featured as a *storySouth* Million Writers Award Notable Story, & his stories & poems have been nominated for the Pushcart Prize, Best Small Fictions, Best Microfiction, Best Of The Net, & the Orison Anthology. He is the series editor of the *Wigleaf* Top 50. He lives in Lafayette, LA & can be found at www.shomedome.com & @laughingyeti

About the Publisher

Thirty West Publishing House

Handmade Chapbooks (and more) since 2015

www.thirtywestph.com / thirtywestph@gmail.com

You should follow us! Consider being a patron?

Review our books on Amazon & Goodreads

@thirtywestph